STONE
STONE COLD FOX TRILOGY

max monroe
New York Times & USA Today Bestselling Author

Stone

Book One in the Stone Cold Fox Trilogy

Published by Max Monroe LLC © 2018, Max Monroe

All rights reserved.

ISBN-13: 978-1986676175
ISBN-10: 198667617X

Without limiting the rights under copyright reserved above, no part of this publication may be reproduced, stored in or introduced into a retrieval system, or transmitted, in any form, or by any means (electronic, mechanical, photocopying, recording, or otherwise) without the prior written permission of both the copyright owner and the above publisher of this book.

This is a work of fiction. Names, characters, places, brands, media, and incidents are either the product of the author's imagination or are used fictitiously. The author acknowledges the trademarked status and trademark owners of various products referenced in this work of fiction, which have been used without permission. The publication/use of these trademarks is not authorized, associated with, or sponsored by the trademark owners.

Editing by Silently Correcting Your Grammar
Formatting by Champagne Book Design
Cover Design by Peter Alderweireld
Photo Credit: iStock Photo

DEDICATIONS

To TUMS and Pepto-Bismol.
Thank you for aiding our digestive systems while Levi and Ivy took us on the emotional ride of our lives.
We needed you. A lot.

To Passion.
Yes, you are not an actual person or thing or anything corporeal, really, but you are the reason Levi and Ivy's story is being told.
Thank you, Passion, you greedy, nagging, beautiful, wonderful, all-consuming,
little asshole.
You sure know how to inspire and drive and motivate us.

And last, but certainly not least.

To Jennifer Lawrence and Emma Stone.
You two are unbelievably talented in your craft.
And, in a lot of ways, you were our muses for Ivy.
Now, with that being said, when do we get to have lunch and be best friends?

STONE
BOOK ONE

Welcome to Cold, Montana, where the town is smaller than a shoebox and their biggest claim to fame is a serial killer.

It's a case that ended in a tragic set of events—one the town would rather forget.

But no one can make tragedy sexy like Hollywood, and whether Levi Fox, one of investigators on the real case, likes it or not, the razzle-dazzle of ready, set, action is coming to Cold.

Worse than that? His captain agreed to make him the liaison for any and all information about his former partner, Grace Murphy.

But Hollywood doesn't know all the details of the real case, and Levi Fox vows to take them to the grave.

Only he and the killer know the truth.

 **Note: As this book is darker in nature, some sensitive scenes and/or subject matter may be present.

CH Warning: Levi and Ivy's story will continue in Book Two—*Cold*.

INTRO

THE NEW YORK CHRONICLE

The Cold-Hearted Killer

Five days ago, a fourth woman went missing in the same small town in Montana where three women have already been found dead in the last seven months. All three bodies were discovered within a six-mile radius.

Although law enforcement officials have been tight-lipped on most of the details, one thing is clear: there's a serial killer in their midst.

September 15th, 2010

COLD—Authorities say just two weeks after a body found in a wooded area inside the small town of Cold, Montana had been identified as the missing twenty-five-year-old woman named Emily Morrow, another woman, twenty-four-year-old Bethany Johnson, has been reported as missing.

This marks the fourth woman who has gone missing in the small, and otherwise sleepy, town of Cold, Montana in the span of seven months.

On the morning of September 10th, twenty-four-year-old Bethany Johnson told her boyfriend she'd be back home in a few hours and was last seen getting into a silver Honda Civic parked outside of her home. Bethany intended to drop by a friend's house located approximately ten minutes away, but she never arrived.

On July 17th, twenty-five-year-old Carly Best's remains were found inside a vacant home. That same day, twenty-seven-year-old Victoria Carson's remains were found in a nearby abandoned barn.

This string of murders seems obtrusive in a town that rarely sees one case, if any, of homicide or manslaughter in a year.

"This is very out of character for our small community," Chief Pulse said during a press conference. "The patterns of these murders, the manner in which they are being committed, along with the similarities between the victims, proves they are not a coincidence. We are dealing with a serial killer here."

"A $5,000 reward is being offered for information about Bethany Johnson," Officer Grace Murphy of the Cold Police Department instructed at a press conference as she held up a picture of the twenty-four-year-old woman. "She is five feet, four inches tall and weighs 130 pounds. She has brown hair, amber eyes, and light skin, with a birthmark on her front right thigh. She also has a butterfly tattoo on her left ankle."

"Please," she added, clearly moved by the uncharacteristic trouble in her town, "anyone with more information regarding Bethany's whereabouts, please come forward so we can find her."

The city's coroner, Dr. Walter Gaskins, has issued autopsy reports on all three victims and confirmed all deaths occurred by strangulation. There are other details within the reports that have not been released to the public yet, but an anonymous inside source has come forward to give us one more, important fact. Carved into the victims' skin with a knife, the killer left one thing behind: **a tiny, broken heart.**

In Cold, Montana, love has started to hurt.

PROLOGUE

Levi
January 3rd, 2016

My fisted hand hovered over the worn wood of Chief Red Pulse's door for one beat, then two—long enough to fill my lungs with much-needed air—and then connected sharply three times.

The chief's call to enter wasn't any less severe than the raps of my knuckles.

"Come in!"

I swallowed and shoved.

The door opened with surprising ease given the dread I felt.

It wasn't that I didn't like Chief Pulse—I did. I'd known the man my entire life and respected him greatly. He was a good man, with good values, and had more time on the force than anyone else.

Seeing as he was pushing seventy-five, that wasn't all that surprising.

But being summoned to his office always felt a little like being called to the principal, even when I hadn't done anything wrong. And today, the timing was horrendously suspicious.

My worst nightmare was scheduled to roll into town soon.

As he was never a man to dance around an issue, his rusty brown eyes didn't waste any time meeting my own. His eyebrows were wild and his clothing slightly sloppy, an appearance I suspected was common for most old men, but his mind was sharp. You could see it in his stare, without question.

Beyond that, I could see his intention, written in the determined gleam and softening wrinkles around the edges—this meeting wasn't going to go my way. I had no way of knowing what he was going to tell me, but I knew, with absolute certainty, I wasn't going to like it.

"Take a seat, Levi," he offered, gesturing to the worn, brown leather chairs in front of his desk.

I glanced their way, and a memory snapped into focus as though it'd happened yesterday. Several memories, actually.

His wife, Margo, had picked those chairs out a good twenty years ago, back when I'd been nothing more than a rebellious kid. My ass had been one with those chairs on more than my fair share of occasions as good-hearted, stern-talking Chief Pulse had read me the riot act.

You better turn your life around, son, he'd told me at the end of nearly every speech. Of course, the beginning and the middle had been filled with a lot more cursing and a little more yelling. But the end, that was where he made it count. And thanks to his unending faith and patience, I had.

Now I stood before him as a man. A coworker.

A cop.

"I'd really rather stand, sir," I deferred. I felt a whole lot less vulnerable if I didn't have furniture inhibiting a quick getaway.

The Chief acquiesced with a nod. "Suit yourself."

I stepped farther into the room then, taking up residence right behind one of those ever-familiar chairs and settling my hands lightly onto the back. The cracked leather scratched at my palms.

"What can I do for you?" I asked outright. I didn't want to wait through pleasantries or speeches, and I didn't want to be in here any longer than I had to be. I felt cagey.

But it wasn't his office, I realized, making me feel edgy. The picture was a whole lot bigger than that. I wanted to be out in the field, on the street—free to move.

I needed the outlet, the unpredictable. I needed to be somewhere where I didn't see *her* everywhere I looked.

He nodded with respect. It took balls to lead a conversation where you wanted it to go rather than let it take you somewhere. Old Red understood that better than nearly anyone I knew, and there was a reason—he'd been the one to teach me that lesson himself.

"The film outfit that's pulling into town…"

I jerked up my chin, my fingers clenching into the leather beneath them, scratchy cracks all but forgotten.

I knew all about the movie they were making in my town—Cold, Montana. I knew the actors they'd hired and the story they meant to tell, and I hated every fucking thing about it. The nightmare I'd suspected brought me in here was starting to feel a little too real.

He couldn't be thinking—

"You're in," he murmured, and everything inside me seized. My heart, my lungs, all of the thoughts in my head—frozen.

"Chief," I whispered, my voice sounding hoarse to even my own ears. This was fucking unbelievable. Ridiculous. Lunacy. He couldn't fucking think for one fucking second I'd be okay with this.

He shook his head and held up a hand, and I did my best to lock it down. My jaw flexed under my frustration's sudden and unyielding pressure.

"You're gonna be the liaison between us and them." My throat burned with disbelief and a million unspoken curses. "I know you've got a sore spot when it comes to this, but the town commission is excited about the profits from this project. They pushed it through with a unanimous vote, and you and I can't do anything about it. It's happening. It deserves some truth, and dammit, Levi, there ain't nobody else."

I shook my head and told him to go fuck himself a thousand times in my head, but he just nodded.

"You know the case, you know Grace, and her family doesn't want anyone to do it but you."

"What if I refuse?" I asked. It was a real option and one I was considering more and more by the minute. I could walk out of here, go about my business, continue my day-to-day, and that stupid movie and its stupid story could go fuck itself.

"Then you'll be fired."

Fine, my inner asshole screamed. *Fire me, then.*

But if there were two things I knew about myself, down to the root, it was this:

I was born to be a cop, and I'd give my life for Cold, Montana.

And someone else already had.

I had no fucking choice.

"When do I start?"

"Day after tomorrow." Red forced a smile. "Silver lining, son. You'll be compensated heavily."

I laughed harshly, and he nodded.

He knew a third thing about me, and so did I.

I didn't give a fuck about the money. I never fucking had.

CHAPTER ONE

Ivy

January 10th, 2016

M Y PHONE RANG THROUGH THE SPEAKERS OF MY RENTAL CAR FOR the fifth time in the last hour, and I sighed. I clutched my hands around the steering wheel in both annoyance and frustration before I tapped the accept button with my right thumb.

"Hey, Mariah," I greeted without even looking at the screen on my dash to see who it was. I knew it would be my manager. Surely, she had something to bitch about. It was her MO.

"You missed a fitting," she said, diving right into what I'd already known.

"I'm aware." I sighed and rolled my eyes toward the sky. "And why aren't you calling Camilla about this? Pretty sure she's the one who handles schedules."

"Because you don't just miss a fitting when a world-renowned designer is making your dress for the fucking Oscars. Do you have any idea how many phone calls I've fielded today regarding this fucking mess?"

"I'm pretty sure my reason for missing the fitting was valid."

"Oh, honey," she said, and a sarcastic laugh escaped her lips. "There is no valid reason for missing a fitting with Christiano LaMoore. Death wouldn't be a valid excuse."

"Stop being so dramatic," I said, and I could only imagine the wrinkles forming between my manager's brows. Beverly Hills probably wouldn't have enough Botox on hand to solve it. "I called Christiano and explained the situation to him," I added by way of calming her down. "He didn't sound upset about it. He completely understood."

"Are you sure about that?" she questioned, her voice rising with each word. "Because I'm sitting here staring at an exclusive interview with Christiano on *Gossip World's* website, and it appears that he wasn't all that understanding."

I scrunched my nose. "What do you mean? What did he say?"

"Something along the lines of your being part of the new epidemic of young and entitled Hollywood actresses."

"That bastard!" I said on a surprised shout. "I told him production was moved up on *Cold* and I had to leave earlier than expected for Montana. It was either I made the fitting and pissed off my director *and* quite possibly got kicked off the job, or I canceled the fitting."

"Well, it looks like he thinks you're full of shit."

"The fact that I've been driving for two hours in the middle-of-nowhere Montana says I'm not," I retorted. "Not to mention, it's literally zero degrees here." I glanced at the temperature on the dashboard just to clarify what I already knew. "I didn't know it was possible to be zero degrees. But it's zero fucking degrees. Trust me, I'd much rather be in LA right now. Although, the traffic isn't so bad here."

I loved living in Los Angeles, but the traffic sucked. And it didn't just suck a little, it sucked a lot. One minute you could be zipping along at a yippee-no-problem-life-is-good kind of pace, and then twenty seconds later, you find yourself squealing to a dead fucking stop. Not to mention, once you actually arrived at your destination, you had to pry your fingers off the steering wheel and look for the nearest stiff drink.

Montana was the exact opposite. I'd driven at least fifteen miles without seeing more than a few semitrucks and maybe one other car on the road. It was damn near eerie how empty the roads were. If I wasn't positive my GPS was leading me exactly where I needed to be, I might've thought I was headed toward something that looked more like *Texas Chainsaw Massacre* than the small town where my next movie would be filmed.

"Well, unless you start kissing Christiano's ass and begging for his forgiveness, I guess you can start looking for a new Oscar-worthy dress."

I sighed. White, luxurious, soft as silk but felt like cotton, the Christiano LaMoore dress was a dream. He was the exact designer most actresses would contemplate giving up their firstborn for. But although I loved designer duds, I wasn't a slave to fashion. Nor would I be apologizing to a man whose ego was apparently bigger than his fashion line's price tags.

"Yeah," I snorted. "Considering I did absolutely nothing wrong, I'd rather remove a limb than ask for forgiveness."

Mariah laughed, finally dropping her tough as nails persona and succumbing to my stubbornness. She knew I wouldn't go back on this—not for a dress to the Oscars, not for a fucking Oscar itself. "I guess I'll start making some phone calls then, huh?"

"Good plan." I smiled. She was a total pain in my ass most days, but when she wasn't acting like such a hard-ass, she was actually a good friend. "And, if you don't mind, find me someone who is up-and-coming and doesn't have a giant, gold-plated, I'm holier than thou stick up their ass."

Lucky for me, I still had a few more months before I needed to worry about being red-carpet ready and had time to shop around.

"I'll see what I can do," she lilted. "Speaking of the Oscars, have you decided who you're bringing with you?"

I was currently single, had zero dating prospects, and my last relationship ended after I found my musician boyfriend with his hands up some groupie's skirt. Obviously, it was an easy answer.

"No one."

"You can't go to the Oscars without a date, Ivy."

"Oh, trust me, I can," I retorted. "I'm a strong, independent female who does not need a man by my side to feel validated. I am woman, hear me roar."

"You're such a pain in my ass," she muttered. "Ms. Hollywood A-Lister with a mile-long list of eligible bachelors trying to score a date with her, and she doesn't want to give anyone the time of day."

"Shall I remind you of the last man on that list I dated?"

"Who? Bradley Romero?"

Gross. He was the most eligible douchebag in Hollywood. One blockbuster movie under his belt and he thought he was God's gift to women.

"Ew. *Hell* no. But he's a perfect example of why I refuse any dating requests that come through my manager."

"Bradley wasn't *that* bad, Ivy."

I snorted. "He is an arrogant asshole, and you and I both know it."

Mariah sighed, and I knew that defeated little sound said everything. She knew I was right about Bradley.

"Give it up, girlfriend. I'm not bringing a date to the Oscars."

"I just want you to be happy," she responded, and I rolled my eyes.

"You want publicity," I retorted.

"That is so not true."

"Oh yes, it is," I responded on a laugh. "But it's okay. I still love you."

"Of course you do," she stated. Just like me, Mariah was a woman who knew her own worth. "Thanks to me, you had a meeting with Hugo Roman, and now, you are the star in his upcoming movie. People are already comparing you to Jodie Foster in *The Silence of the Lambs*."

Hugo Roman was one of Hollywood's most highly coveted directors. His name was synonymous with powerhouses like Spike Lee and Steven Spielberg. If you had the opportunity to be in one of his movies, you dropped everything and did it no matter what sacrifices you had to make.

And Mariah was right about getting me the meeting, but securing opportunities for me was her job. Trust me, she was compensated heavily, and she'd have a much easier time spending that money than trying to trade for goods with a pat on the back.

Also, *Jodie Foster*? Jesus, no pressure or anything.

I wasn't new to the Hollywood game, and I already had one Academy Award nomination under my belt, but having my name anywhere near a legend like that was intimidating. And this movie—*Cold*—well, it wasn't the kind of film you walked onto the set of without being prepared.

The instant I'd read the screenplay, I'd known I was born to play this role. It was that gut instinct, that "this is so right" feeling that would keep me from folding under the insane pressure.

"Are you still there?" Mariah's voice pulled me from my thoughts.

"Yeah…I'm just trying to figure out where in Beverly Hills I'll have them put your gilded gold statue and if it will be thanks enough for you."

"Let me think on that some more and get back to you." She laughed, and I grinned at the windshield.

"Yeah, okay. I'm going to go now before you start asking for an expense account at Tiffany's. Bye, Mariah."

I ended the call and followed my GPS as he directed me to take the next exit ramp. Crossing over two completely empty lanes, I was flying high and fast once I hit the even more open back roads of Montana.

Cold, Montana: 4 miles, the sign read, and internally, I rejoiced. I was ready to get out of this rental and into the house I'd be calling home for the next four months.

With the snow-covered mountains in my periphery and another quick glance to the neon green temperature on my dashboard, I verified the city lived up to its name. It was fucking *cold*. Negative one degrees, to be exact.

The now quiet car became far too silent, and I turned up the radio and quickly found myself bopping up and down to Rhianna's voice singing "This is What You Came For."

I smiled in relief as the road yawned wide before me, only a light smattering of traffic in the distance.

A quick glance to the clock told me if I moved my ass, I could be sitting in a hot bath in less than twenty minutes. It was only a quarter after two in the afternoon, and I didn't have any real obligations until tomorrow morning.

I pressed the pedal to the metal and sped up my pace, weaving in and out of what little traffic peppered the roadway. Montana probably wasn't used to LA's version of driving, but I figured all of three semis and a beat-up Chevy pickup wouldn't pay my hurried tempo too much attention.

Flashes of red and blue bounced off my side mirror and into my eyes at the same time a sudden blast from a siren filled my ears.

I glanced up into the rearview mirror and saw the familiar sight of a police cruiser following closely behind me. The blue and red lights on top of the roof flashed obnoxiously as if to say *"Somebody was paying attention! You totally fucked up!"*

Considering I was going seventy in a fifty, I really had fucked up.

Shit. Shit. Shit.

Welcome to fucking Cold, Montana, Ivy.

"Son of a nutcracker," I muttered to myself and pulled off to the side of the road. As I came to a dead stop and put my car in park, I wracked my brain for some sort of excuse to get me out of a speeding ticket.

While I waited for the officer to get out of his cruiser and make his approach, I quickly narrowed down my possible options.

"I'm sorry, officer, I'm from LA. I didn't realize the speed limit was only fifty here. I thought it was seventy."

No, that wouldn't work. That only made me sound like an idiot. And the whole LA bit would probably only piss him off more.

"I know I was speeding, but I have diarrhea."

Ew, that was too gross. And Jesus, if he somehow recognized me and let that white lie hit the tabloids, Mariah would be uberpissed. Forget Beverly Hills—there wouldn't be enough Botox in the *world* to fix the wrinkles my fictional stomach problems would cause.

I looked toward the center console and saw a half-empty bottle of water in the cupholder.

What about "I have to pee?" Will that work?

The sound of the cop's door slamming shut filled my ears, and any rational thought flitted out the window. Panic took over. Grabbing the water bottle in my hands, I tried to discreetly unscrew the cap and pour the rest of it onto my lap.

But before I could get the bottle back into the cupholder, my time was up and the male police officer rapped on my window with his knuckles. *Busted.*

With dread, I rolled down my window to open the lines of communication between us, and my jaw hit the top of my door at the sight.

Midnight black hair, tanned skin, and dusky blue-green eyes the color of the deepest part of the Caribbean stared back at me. I couldn't stop myself from doing a double take, and on the second go-round I noted his prominent cheekbones, his well-defined nose and chin, and one tattoo tucked away on the inside of his left arm. It was too intricate to inspect closely, but it was well done. No broken ink-pen, home-tattoo garbage for this guy. And good God, his arms—well, actually his whole fucking body.

And how in the hell was he so tan? Surely, people didn't actually go out in the sun in this town. At least not in the dead of fucking winter. Limbs would freeze off in these temperatures. Blue balls would be an actual real-life diagnosis.

He cleared his throat, and I quickly moved my gaze back up to his eyes.

Which, to be honest, wasn't any better. They were the most vivid, all-consuming eyes I'd ever seen. They had the power to draw you in like a magnet and never release you from their powerful hold.

Somehow, someway, I had just been pulled over by the hottest police officer on the planet.

"Are you doing anything in particular with that water bottle?" he asked, his full lips set in a straight line. He was hot, but goddamn, he was serious. Any more hostility on his face and it might just up and shatter.

Instantly, I looked down at the now empty bottle in my hands and the giant wet spot on my jeans. *Shit. This looks incriminating....*

My heart raced inside my chest as I tried to find an explanation for why I'd poured a bottle of water on myself.

Fucking hell. Mariah will kill me if I end up getting arrested for a fake-piss stunt like this.

"Uh…N-no," I stuttered. "I was, uh…I was just trying to take a quick drink, and yeah, I guess my nerves got the best of me."

Hard-ass showed no signs of sympathy.

"Do you know why I pulled you over?"

I didn't think the real truth held merit, but a vague version of it seemed like the best way to go now that I knew he was unfazed by pants that looked like I'd pissed myself. This guy didn't seem like he'd award me any points for creativity. "Because I was going a little fast?"

"A little fast?" he repeated, one of his long-fingered hands reaching out to rest on my window sill. He was tall, over six foot by my estimation, and he had to lean down to look me directly in the eye. "You were going seventy-three in a fifty."

"Wait a minute," I protested despite his authoritative tone, pointing to the dashboard. "My speed checker thingy said I was going seventy. Not seventy-three."

For the first time, his granite face showed signs of life, just one pointed corner of his full lips turning to move upward. "So, you *were* aware that you were going more than just a *little* fast?"

Shit.

"I was aware I was going *seventy*, not seventy-three."

"So, you admit to going over twenty miles per hour over the speed limit?"

Shit, shit, shit. Good Lord, was this guy a human lie detector? And why was my brain not working at full capacity?

"Wait…what?" I questioned by way of tossing out my "I'm a total idiot, but I don't want you to know I'm an idiot" card.

"You just said you thought you were going seventy—"

"I *know* I was going seventy."

"Great. I'll be sure to note your admission of guilt on the ticket."

This is not going the direction I wanted it to go...

"Wait—"

"License and registration, please."

"Are you really going to write me a ticket?" I questioned as I rummaged through my purse and the glove box and, eventually, found the things he'd requested.

"Well," he said and pointed to his badge with his pen. "Seeing as you broke the law, it's kind of my job to write you a ticket."

Is this guy serious right now?

Angry vibes filled the space between us, both his and a whole shit-ton of mine, but I was an actor. I made a lot of money pretending to be something I wasn't, so for now, I could pretend to be something other than *pissed*. I went with pitiful. "You're really going to give me a ticket? I mean, can't you just let me off with a warning," I begged. "I've just had a shit kind of day, and I'm just trying to get to…" I paused immediately before the rest of the sentence came out of my mouth.

Surely, using my "I'm in need of a hot bath" excuse wasn't going to help in this scenario.

"You're trying to get to where?" He raised a challenging brow, any and all signs of good-nature gone again. I was starting to hate how fucking handsome he was without a smile. Most people really needed a smile to transform their face into something spectacular. This guy didn't need shit.

"To an appointment," I responded, and his lips thinned. He knew I was lying.

"An appointment? What kind of appointment?"

"A hot bath appointment," I muttered, finally realizing I just needed to shut up.

I looked down at his chest to find his last name inscribed into a plate on his navy uniform shirt, just above his right pec. **Fox,** it read. Déjà vu hit me hard. I'd heard that name before. I had no idea where the familiarity came from, but it sure as hell rang some distant bells of recognition.

And seriously? Officer fucking *Fox*.

Of course, that was his last name. That was totally a hot guy last name.

"Okay," he said and glanced down at my driver's license in his hands, "Ms. Ivy Stone." His body froze then, his eyes moving from the license to me and back again. A little bloom of hope sprung to life in my stomach. *Maybe he recognizes my name. Maybe I'm going to get off with a warning, after all.*

I watched him closely for a sign that he was cracking, but all I got was a kick to the gut.

Hate, pure and infinite, colored his pretty eyes with smoke as he looked me over again. I was used to scrutiny—but not this kind. This was calculated and venomous and amplified to the nth degree. His opinion of me was undeniable. Officer Fox looked at my pretty red hair, bright green eyes, and long legs, did the math of putting them all together, and came up with disgust.

"Sit tight," he ground out. "I'll be back."

"Are you really going to write me a ticket?" I asked just before he could take a real step, and his body turned back in slow motion.

My pulse thrummed in my neck as he bent down again and speared me with a coldness stronger than the nonexistent degrees outside.

"Are you *really* going to ask me to let you out of a ticket because you were driving twenty miles over the speed limit so you didn't miss your so-called *appointment*? Are you *that* entitled?"

What. A. Dick.

Silently, I searched for the words, scrambled to come up with something to explain to this man that he had me all wrong, but it was no use. Officer I'm Too Sexy for My Clothes had already made up his mind about me.

Luckily, hate wasn't exclusive. I could make up my mind about him right back.

I watched as he strolled back to his police cruiser, clouded in untouchable power and douchebaggery. And I decided right then that for as long as I had to be here in this godforsaken icy tundra hell, I'd make sure Officer Fox and I saw as little of each other as humanly possible.

CHAPTER TWO

Levi

A SOFT RIPPLE OF EXCITEMENT TITTERED THROUGH THE ONLY BAR IN town—Ruby Jane's—as I stepped inside the door. It didn't take more than a couple of seconds for all those whispers to roll into silence, though.

It wasn't surprising given the facts, what with every-fucking-body knowing everybody else's business in Cold's tiny pot of people. They knew me—and they had since birth—and they knew my story. And now they knew, with exquisite detail, the part of that story that had made it all the way to Hollywood. In turn, Hollywood had made its way to us.

I guessed the buzz of fame and chaos of a premier film operation in town had everyone excited—until my buzzkill ass had walked through the door.

I ignored their stares and expressive eyes and made my way to the most important part of Ruby Jane's—the alcohol. After the day I'd had today, I needed a drink.

Fucking Ivy Stone. She had a mane of red hair that would rival a lion and a superiority complex big enough to fill this entire bar. And she'd been so desperate to get out of getting a ticket from me that she'd attempted to fake a scenario where she'd lost control of her bladder.

I bet she's used to getting her way.

A tiny smirk pursed my lips. Well, she hadn't gotten her way today. I'd made sure of that.

Neither did you, a mutinous, sadistic voice inside me taunted. Chief's edict this morning was still in full effect, and I couldn't do a damn thing to change it. I was the official fucking liaison for a Hollywood film I wanted nothing to do with.

"Jack," I ordered from Lou, bar manager and bartender since his wife Celia had died of cancer three years ago. He'd been the bartender for years, but something about being home after his wife passed lost its appeal. With the number of hours he spent here, stepping up to be the manager too just made sense.

I settled my ass onto one of the high-backed stools and dropped my keys onto the bar. Lou's eyes were lifeless and, unlike the others, his curiosity nonexistent. He got my drink with practiced ease, but he didn't have anything else to offer. I didn't blame him, especially with the experiences he'd had in the past. And tonight, I wouldn't have wanted it any different.

"Take these," I told him, shoving my keys to his side of the sticky bartop surface as he set down a tall glass of Jack Daniel's, cut by nothing more than a cube of ice. I planned on being just shy of forgetting my name by the time I got ready to stumble out of here, and I didn't want even a hint of lingering temptation to drive.

I wanted to get blitzed out of my mind, but I wasn't suicidal.

Just a quiet night of inebriation. That was all I needed.

Mary Lynn Tenner had different ideas. The stool next to mine scraped loudly across the beat-up wood floor as she took a seat and leaned in to crowd me. It wasn't subtle, and neither were her tits. Any higher and they'd be around her ears.

"Good to see you out, Levi," she said, her vowels rolling with the sweet promise of all her loose pussy had to offer.

And trust me, it was fucking loose. She'd seen a hell of a lot more dick than I had, and I had one attached to my body.

"You looking for some company?"

I shook my head and looked into the amber-brown liquid in my glass.

"Just here to drink."

"Shame," she pouted, leaning even closer, so much that the top swells of her breasts rubbed lewdly against my arm. "If you change your mind, let me know."

Instead of answering, I picked up the tumbler off of the bar and tossed it back, downing damn near the whole glass in one go, and set it back with a smack. Lou didn't even look up as he picked up the bottle of Jack and poured until the glass was full again.

My vision tunneled, and the room disappeared as I did it again and again. Rinse and repeat. Mary Lynn disappeared at some point—I knew by the lack of offensive perfume clogging my nostrils—but I didn't really care.

It was just me and my glass, sliding further and further into numbness.

I had no idea how long I sat there before my best friend Jeremy was beside me, one hand to my shoulder, the other prying the glass from my hand. "I think that's enough for tonight."

"Jeremy!" I greeted happily, like seeing him was a surprise. And, in a way, it was. Jeremy had a wife and two daughters and too much self-respect to spend his nights in Ruby Jane's getting shitfaced. "Wha' er you doin' here, bro?" I slurred.

"I'm here for you, buddy."

"Nahh, Jer. I'm good. I am goo-ood."

He nodded obediently. "I know you are, Levi. But I miss you. How about we go back to your place and chat?"

"Thas a good idea. Old Red chatted me this mornin'. Did he tell you?" Jeremy shook his head. At least, I think he did. I rambled on anyway. "You're lookin' at the lee-ay-zon. Official. Me and Hollywood and a fucking movie. Can you believe that?" I patted the bar around me. "I jus' gotta fine my keys."

Lou held them up behind the bar. "You gave them to me, Levi. I'll hold on to them for now."

I nodded. Lou was such a nice guy. So nice and lonely and always fucking giving me all the booze I wanted. I liked him.

"I'll come back for his car after I get him home," Jeremy said.

"Goooooood I-dea, guys!" I said on a shout and attempted to pat Jeremy on the shoulder. I missed. Or he moved. I didn't know which. But I knew I shouldn't be driving any-fucking-where.

I stood up and stumbled a little, but Jer, the fucking best friend ever, he was there to catch me. He wound my arm around his shoulder after that.

"You're the bessst. Do you know that, Jer?" I asked as he walked me out the door. There weren't any prying eyes this time, though. They'd long since gone home.

"I know, Lee. You're not bad yourself."

Everything in me turned melancholy as the cold wind slapped at my cheeks. "I'm the worst," I admitted. "Draggin' you out here in the freezingness. The frozen? The fucking snowww!" I shouted at the end.

Jeremy patted my hand that dangled over his shoulder. "It's okay. Living with three girls, they've always got the fucking heat turned up to the Hades setting. I needed a little cold air."

With some creative maneuvering, he got the passenger door to his

Yukon open and poured me into the seat. I snuggled into the soft leather and closed my eyes.

Red hair and green eyes singed the backs of my eyelids as vividly as a picture.

"She's pretty," I mumbled as Jeremy muscled my legs into the space in front of the seat.

"Who is?" he asked.

Though I heard the question, I didn't have time to answer. I was already asleep.

CHAPTER THREE

Ivy

"Are you all settled in?" my mom's voice filled my ear. At twenty-eight years old, I still found comfort in hearing her voice when I was away on location. I guessed, deep down, we were all just kids at heart who never really grew out of needing our moms.

"Yep," I responded into the receiver as I watched the coffee machine brew my favorite beverage in the whole wide world. Helen Stone was an early riser, thank God. If she wasn't, with my call times and hectic schedule, I feared I'd never really get to talk to her.

"So, what's it like out there in Montana?" she asked. I nearly laughed. Montana was such a stark contrast to home, I wasn't even sure she'd understand if I tried to explain it.

California sure as shit didn't have snow, or ridiculously handsome alphas with police badges and bad attitudes driving around—or, if it did, I'd yet to meet them—but that was the least of it. The entire way of life—the pace, the relationships, the things they valued—was completely different.

Explaining all of that this early in the morning seemed daunting, though, so I stuck with the basics.

"Trust me, neither you nor Dad would enjoy the weather here."

Both my parents were Californians through and through. Born and raised in the Golden State, they'd lived on the West Coast their whole lives, and their love for all of the amazing things it had to offer was why they'd stayed put in LA. They'd retired and sold off the small Stone family business—a few very successful secondhand, vintage clothing and antique shops—a couple of years ago, but I hadn't seen even a hint of temptation to wander. Everything they wanted was right there.

"Yeah, you're probably right." A soft laugh left her lips. "I'll take sun and sand over snow and ice any day of the week."

"Me too," I said. A smile lifted the corners of my mouth as I poured myself a cup of coffee. "All right, well, I need to get to work. Love you, Mom. And don't forget to say hi to Dad for me, okay?"

"Love you too, Ivy," she said, and my heart squeezed. Those words from my mom would never, *ever* get old. After we said our goodbyes, I ended the call and slid my phone back into the pocket of my silk robe.

With a hot cup of coffee in my hands and the morning sun still tucked away behind a carbon winter sky, I sat down at the kitchen table inside my new humble abode and stared down at the first page of the script.

COLD

Screenplay by June Gatto

Based on the real-life events of the Cold-Hearted Killer

Trigate Films

Imaginext Entertainment

Today was day numero uno for *Cold*. We wouldn't start actual production for another two weeks, but today was the beginning of my official preparation. Technically, I guessed my formal prep had started on the drive in when I'd outright refused to be chauffeured into town and demanded that production provide me with a suitable rental. Something like Grace Murphy would have driven.

I'd briefly read through the screenplay prior to my initial meeting with Hugo Roman, but that had been over six months ago. I still remembered the basics, mostly revolving around Grace Murphy's character, but the bulk of it was just fuzzy details now.

This movie, and the true-life events it was based on, was not something I wanted to take lightly. What had happened inside the city limits of this small town, and the tragic events that had occurred at the hands of a ruthless serial killer, was downright shocking. I'd heard about the Cold-Hearted Killer—a man who'd murdered because he'd hated love—in the news. I'd even remembered some of the other details surrounding the case, including the disturbing signature of a tiny heart he'd carved into his victims' skin.

But my job for the next fourteen days was to put myself into my character's shoes as much as I possibly could before filming started.

Grace Murphy had been one of the detectives on the case. She had been young, late-twenties, and if it hadn't been for her act of bravery, Walter Donald Gaskins might still be prowling the streets for new unsuspecting female victims.

I needed to get inside Detective Grace Murphy's head. I needed to experience what her life would've been like when this case had been the top priority on her desk. I needed to eat, sleep, and breathe her life.

I wouldn't say method acting was something I utilized for every film, but for *Cold*, it was a necessity. I couldn't live up to the part without truly trying to understand Grace.

And some of my biggest heroes had utilized method acting. Hilary Swank had lived full time as a man for weeks before the shoot for *Boys Don't Cry*. During the production of *Taxi Driver*, Robert DeNiro actually drove a cab around New York City to get ready for his role.

And don't even get me started on Daniel Day-Lewis. He had proven time and time again that method acting only encouraged an authentic, award-worthy performance. There wasn't one single work of his that didn't make my heart race and skin tingle.

I flipped through the script, glancing briefly at various scenes until I finished my first cup of coffee. I didn't make it very far into the story, but I had a full two weeks to get acquainted. There was no pressure to rush it.

I didn't have any time left this morning anyway. I had to get ready to leave. First stop of the day: Cold, Montana Police Department.

I had an eight thirty a.m. meeting with the Chief.

My phone pinged as I pulled into the small parking lot of the Cold police station. Once I situated my rental in a spot, I shut off the engine and checked my messages.

Mariah: I've just been told you are wandering around that god-awful frozen tundra without any security. Tell me I've been misinformed...

I rolled my eyes and typed out a quick response.

Me: I don't need security, Mariah. It would make me a spectacle in this small town.

I needed to blend in to my surroundings, not stand out like a Hollywood diva.

Mariah: IVY. I am not okay with this.

The truth of the matter was I'd reached the level of success where having a security detail follow me around wasn't out of the norm. To be honest, it all felt pretty weird to me and seemed to be occurring more and more frequently.

But Cold, Montana was a small town in every aspect of the word. Their population had all of 12,000, which was peanuts compared to the over four million people living inside the city limits of Los Angeles.

I probably needed a parka, thick gloves, and wool socks, but I did not need security.

Me: This town is the size of your thumbnail. Trust me, I don't need security. Does it help to know I'm literally standing outside of the police station right now?

Mariah: Ugh. A little. But I still think you should have security with you. Your stalker was never arrested.

She had a point about the stalker, but that guy was *literally* over a thousand miles away now. And since I wasn't the only Hollywood actress he had been stalking, I figured he'd just keep sending the same creepy, love-profession-filled letters to my PO Box or find someone else to occupy his time with while I was out of the state.

Which…hey, sorry, whoever that turns out to be.

But it still meant it wouldn't be me. I'd officially left his district.

And he, whoever my so-called stalker was, hadn't been much of a threat. Just a creepy annoyance.

The soft exhale of air from my lungs left my lips and billowed out from my face in a small cloud. I shivered, realizing the car had grown noticeably colder since I'd shut off the engine. Not only did I need to seek the much warmer environment of the police station, but I needed to make sure I was on time for my meeting with the chief.

Me: I'll be fine, Mariah. Promise. I'll talk to you later, okay? I gotta run to a meeting.

Mariah: If anything weird happens, you better fucking let me and Camilla know about it. Otherwise, I'm telling Jason about the Cristiano fiasco.

Jason Hawk was a bloodhound. I mean, not literally. Literally, he was my agent and, as such, being able to scent out the blood of the weak was a commendable quality. That didn't mean I wanted him riding *my* ass though.

Me: *Aye-aye, captain.*

Mariah might worry too much, but I could deal with her. I made a mental note to keep her in the loop should the need arise.

I shoved my phone into my purse, *after* turning it to silent, and hopped out of my rental, heading toward the entrance of the station. The flat heels of my boots pushed into the soft snow and crunched against the gravel below it with each step.

Once my fingers met the cool metal of the handle on the glass front door, I found myself face-to-face with an inside view of Cold's police station.

I was all too prepared for chaos, action, *something* that resembled the scenes I'd conjured in my mind, but there was relatively little hustle going on when I stepped inside the police station at a quarter after eight. With blond-gray hair and muddy brown eyes, the receptionist was still slipping into her chair behind her desk, a black mug of coffee steaming in front of her. Through the glass behind her, I could see that ninety percent of the whopping five desks in the pit were empty.

Wait? That would mean there was half a guy, wouldn't it? Whatever, I'm bad at math. There's only one cop working.

Being a woman of Hollywood, I had been imagining mayhem and phones ringing off the hook, guys grabbing their guns and heading out the door in a hurry, and loud, intense chatter. My expectations for crime activity first thing in the morning on a Monday were apparently too high.

"Hi," I murmured softly, trying not to startle the woman as she put the mug to her lips to take an audible slurp. "I'm—"

"Ivy Stone," she finished for me, just barely peeking up over the edge of her hot beverage.

Amusement curled the edges of my mouth like a ribbon. "Yeah. That's me."

Her smirk was mocking as she set the cup down and stood up, hands planted wide on the desk in front of her. "Oh, honey. I know." Slowly and purposefully, she dragged her eyes down the line of my entire body and back up again. "You stick out like a sore thumb."

I surveyed my outfit, something simple I'd thrown on before leaving the house this morning without much thought, this time with an editing eye. All black in color, my cashmere sweater dress hung to mid-thigh, its hem just above the tops of my suede, flat-heeled boots. The inch of skin left between, I'd concealed underneath thick black tights to ward off the cold, and I'd undone my belted Zac Veeson coat as soon as I'd stepped inside.

The corners of the receptionist's eyes crinkled as I moved my gaze from my outfit to hers—wearing a heavy oatmeal-colored, cable-knit sweater, jeans, and snow boots, she was clearly, of the two of us, the native Montana woman.

Internally, I winced. I had a little more work to do if I was going to truly assimilate myself into the Cold, Montana lifestyle and Grace Murphy's shoes.

"Whoops," I muttered.

"I'm Mona," the receptionist said, her smile growing into something genuinely likable at my affable attitude. Obviously, she was expecting the prissy Hollywood A-lister to be confrontational, but I had neither the will nor the inclination. She was right; I'd overdone it. "You'll get the hang of it. Trust me, a couple of times of trudging through the snow, and you'll have no choice."

I brightened with the glow of her reassurance.

A gust of bitter wind caught me by surprise as the front door opened behind me. I curled the edges of my coat closer and squinted into the sun to see the new arrival.

Wearing khaki pants tucked into untied boots and a heavy work coat, the older man yanked his bright orange knit cap off of his head and stomped his feet on the rug to clear them of snow and crud. He had unruly eyebrows and the hairdo to match, and a puff of hot breath made a cloud in the cold air in front of him.

"Hey, Red," Mona said from behind me. "This here's Ivy Stone. Here for your meeting."

Red's gaze shifted to me, and his wind-whipped face melted into a soft smile. His beefy hand felt work-worn as I took it in mine and shook. "Hey there, Ivy. I'm Red. Or Chief Pulse. Call me whatever you like, darlin'."

It was the strangest thing, my cheeks flushing under his kindness. He wasn't attractive and I didn't know him from Adam, but something about the way he looked directly at me, like he could really see me, hit me right in the chest. In Hollywood, most people watched you with one eye, while they kept themselves open for someone better with the other.

I didn't have time to linger in the awkwardness and make a fool of myself, though, because his attention went back to Mona immediately.

"Levi in yet?" he asked.

"Nope," Mona answered. "But Nick got a call from Jeremy last night."

I watched avidly as the chief's face turned downright gloomy, from soft curves to hard lines in less than a second. I fought the urge to step back and settled for crossing my arms over my chest.

"Great. Just send him in when he gets here."

A bud of curiosity over their discussion threatened to bloom, but Red blocked out the light before it could get anywhere by turning back to me. "Come on, Ivy. Come on in my office. Surely, there's a pot of coffee on by now too."

"There is," Mona assured, lifting her cup as evidence.

"Thank God," Red grumbled, stomping toward the glass door behind her and yanking it open. Mona jerked her chin, and I jumped into action.

Right, I'm supposed to follow.

Hustling into a quick jog, I caught the door the chief was holding and followed him through into the mostly dead space. He didn't look back as he trudged toward his office, and I didn't offer any witty conversation. His mood had taken a somewhat dark turn.

Unzipping his coat as we stepped into his office, Red tossed his hat into the chair he had in the back corner and offered me a seat with a mumbled, "Have at it."

The chairs in front of his desk were well worn with heavy use, and the wood of his desk was chipped at the corners. His space wasn't meant to be pretty, but with a nearly two-foot pile of files on one side of his desk, it was fairly obvious it was useful.

Silence descended and I squirmed. As a personal principle, when I did things, I made sure I didn't leave room for error. I studied and plotted and strategized. I dug into the recesses of a character and pulled my motivation from reality.

But today, I wasn't in control. It was up to the department to provide me with what they saw fit, and any holes left in the fabric of my research when they were done were my responsibility to sew closed.

I had no way of knowing how open to questions they'd be or how willing they'd be to delve into the mistakes and faults of a good friend.

Grace had been a member of their team, and I was just an outsider.

I didn't like the uncertainty of it all.

"Can I go get you a cup of coffee while you get settled?" I offered as he hung his coat on the black, iron rack and shuffled through the papers on his desk without much finesse. They fluttered and flopped, and the stack in the corner was reminiscent of the Leaning Tower of Pisa.

I wasn't sure exactly what had him so riled, but I'd gotten a glimpse of the easygoing guy he could be and wanted him back.

He paused at the end of my question, some of his frustration melting right away. The rest clung to his eyes like a ghost on his soul. "That'd be lovely, Ivy. Don't mean to offend you with my mood. It's just…complicated."

I nodded even though I didn't have the first fucking clue what he was talking about. Frankly, I wasn't sure I wanted to. The man had demons in his eyes—big ones.

Pulling my coat from my shoulders, I draped it over the chair in his office and headed back out in search of the coffeepot.

It didn't take long to find, right across the room in the center of the counter. Cops apparently liked their coffee—which was good. That was one thing I wouldn't have any trouble getting into character for.

I had the pot in my hand and a healthy pour started into the mug labeled "Red" when the glass door opened, and the jerk cop who'd given me a ticket yesterday walked in.

He looked bad—the worst I imagined a guy as attractive as him ever did. Red-rimmed, bloodshot eyes and clammy skin, he'd lived a year in only a day's time.

But by some sort of voodoo magic, the man still managed to pull it off.

Call me clichéd, but I had a thing for alphas.

And Officer Fox was alpha to the max. You could see it in his strong jaw, the powerful way he carried himself, and the way his midnight blue eyes exuded sex and sin and control.

Hell, at first, I had the ridiculous urge to make him a cup of coffee and offer him some ibuprofen, but I quickly thought better of it. He might've been a hot as fuck alpha cop, even when he was so obviously hungover, but he was also the dick who welcomed me to Cold, Montana with a speeding ticket.

Without warning, piercing pain coated the skin of my hand and made me jump as the dumb, distracted version of me poured steaming hot coffee up and over the lip of the mug until it ran onto my skin like a glove.

"Shit!"

Officer Fox's gaze came to me, a mean smile livening the dead lines of his eyes as he took in my disaster.

He didn't hesitate to bask in my agony. "Must be a habit of yours."

My eyebrows pinched both in pain and confusion as I shuffled to the sink, dropped the offending mug with a crash, and turned on the cold tap full bore. It soothed the sting on the surface, but it didn't stop the pulsing pain inside.

Christ. *Ow.*

"What?" I asked like a fool, glancing up from the stark white singed skin of my hand and into his deep sapphire eyes.

He jerked his head at my mess, his features almost shockingly devoid of sympathy. Since they were vibrant and supple in all the ways that counted, I figured he had to work at making them appear that severe. "Always pouring shit all over yourself."

Anger, hot and spicy, filled my mouth, its intensity momentarily stronger than the pain. "You *asshole.*"

Full lips pulled back to bare his teeth as he spat his next words. "Better an asshole than a stuck-up bitch—"

"Levi!" Chief Pulse yelled from the doorway of his office, his voice hard and unyielding. "In here! Now!" Head swinging across the room, he speared the only other officer on duty with hard eyes. "Help Ivy, Glen. Make sure she doesn't need a doctor."

The only other man in the room pushed up from his seat, clumsy legs tangling with each other as he tried to escape the web of furniture. He had on a Cold Police uniform, and it wasn't too hard to deduce his name was Glen.

"I'm fine," I said confidently. Actually injured or not, there was no fucking way I was going to the hospital. The last thing I needed on my first official day in town was that kind of attention.

Despite my assurance, Glen crossed the room the rest of the way in a hurry and took my hand in his to survey. He didn't move it out from underneath the tap, and for that I was thankful, but he did a thorough inspection nonetheless.

"Looks like some minor burns, but nothing that won't heal."

I nodded with an easiness I didn't feel. My heart was pounding from the encounter and all of the unexercised anger it had produced. Fucking hell, I wanted to let that arrogant asshole have it. Chief Pulse had intervened in our exchange too fucking soon as far as I was concerned.

"I'll check our first aid kit. See if we have any salve in it," Glen offered. I took a deep breath to calm down before answering on a whisper.

"Thanks."

As soon as he stepped away, I peeked through my curtain of falling hair, eager to see what was going on in the office with Officer Levi Fox.

He was the one they'd been talking about this morning, and he obviously had a big fucking chip on his shoulder. I wondered if it would hurt worse than normal if I punched him in it.

His taut back the only thing of him I could see, I watched as his shoulders bunched, the chief's mouth moving a mile a minute.

I was nearly desperate to hear what was being said, but no matter how hard I strained, the most I could make out was a muffled rumble.

CHAPTER FOUR

Levi

"WHAT THE HELL IS WRONG WITH YOU?" CHIEF SHOUTED. His voice was loud, but honestly, his body language was doing most of the yelling. Wild arms swung out from his bulging neck, and all one hundred and ninety pounds of him were poised forward, ready to break my bones with a tad more attentiveness than a quick snap.

"Do you get some kind of pleasure from being a goddamn idiot?"

"Chief—"

"Shut up! I don't wanna hear any-fucking-thing you could be thinking right now."

The beat of my heart turned caustic. Bitter excuses and unfounded insults raced through my head, and it was on the tip of my tongue to tell him he was the one who was asking fucking questions—but I thought better of it at the last minute.

Always perceptive, he read my mind anyway.

"They're rhetorical, asswipe. I mean, Jesus Christ, you look like a sack of warm dog shit from your little trip to the bottom of the bottle last night."

My jaw flexed at the news that he'd heard about last night. A picture of the chain of human telephone formed clearly in my mind. *Jeremy is friends with Mona's husband, Nick.* "Jeremy—"

"Is a good fucking friend, so you keep your shit-talking mouth shut. I think you said quite e-fucking-nough when you came in here spewing hate at a woman you don't even know."

The f-bombs were flowing like water from his lips. It was his ultimate tell. Old Red wasn't just a tad pissed; he was outright furious.

"I know her," I contested. Her lead foot had introduced us.

You could see the kind of woman she was in every stupid stitch of her designer clothing. You could see it in her mossy, catlike eyes. *I* could see it in the way she held herself like she owned everything around her.

Lush lips, bright green eyes, and a body that could make a man weep, Ivy Stone was beautiful; I'd give her that. But none of that shit mattered to me.

I didn't want anything to do with her.

Yeah, but you don't have a say in the matter.

Worn and brittle, Red's voice lost some of the volume but none of the grit. "You don't know her. You're all twisted up in your head, so much so you can't see past your thick fucking skull."

Mention of my head made it pound with more than just my hangover. My arms felt heavy, and my legs felt weak. I knew blood flowed quickly and reliably through my veins, but for the way I ached, they may as well have been dry.

I hurt. All over. Couldn't he see that?

This whole film liaison bullshit was the fancy, slow, and excruciating version of a knife carving me up from the inside out. It might have only been a day since the chief told me I had no choice in the matter, but I already had enough memories consuming me to be considered an actual haunted landmark.

"You need to find someone else to do this," I whispered. Pain and poison seeped out of me and spilled into the space between us. "Can't you see what this is doing to me? And the fucking film hasn't even started yet," I added by way of a mutter, more to myself than him.

"You're doin' it to yourself," he said softly. I could feel the rough edges of his declaration as it scraped across my skin. All of his bark was gone, but his decision was resolute. I *was* doing this—even if it killed me.

"Now, get yourself together. We're gonna go out there and check on that girl, and I swear to God, you say one fucking thing I don't like, and I'm gonna feed you your balls for breakfast."

Hands in fists and teeth clenched so hard they'd be worn clean away in an hour, I gritted out my answer. The words tasted sour. "Yes. Sir."

Chief Pulse moved to the door, but I stayed rooted to the spot as surely as if my feet had actually attached. As soon as he was out of sight, I closed my eyes, took a deep breath, and then, finally, with sheer force of will and some emotional cutting shears, followed him.

Visions of days past clutched at my chest tightly as I cleared the threshold of the office and saw her there, perched on the edge of Glen's desk, wild red hair covering the entirety of her face while she looked down at her hand. The skin where she'd burned herself was red and angry, and her knee bounced—tiny, fluttery motions—as Glen rubbed the inflammation with cream.

Guilt over my callous disregard for her injury and the lingering Jack Daniel's churned and mixed in my stomach. I struggled against the impulse to throw up the rotten combination and stepped closer to the huddle at Glen's desk.

Ivy's head came up as I got near. Her body tightened and her eyes dulled, all green glitter and sparkle gone.

Translation: I wasn't welcome in her personal space.

As much as I wanted to, I couldn't fully blame her.

"Are you okay?" I asked, somehow finding a way to hustle the words through the fire in my throat.

Harsh words and pithy comments hung precariously on the tip of her tongue—I could tell. But with just one glance to Red, she held them back.

Instead, she gave me an answer. And it was genuine, every bit of it, as well as cool and detached. "I'm fine. I doubt they'll be planning my funeral anytime soon."

As much as the words were innocent, harmless filler to her, they were like a goddamn bullet to the chest for me. *Funeral.* That word was associated with memories I didn't want to lose myself in. It was all too fucking painful, and the chief noticed and moved to defuse the situation.

"Look, why don't we call it for today? Ivy should at least get someone to look at her hand. And you should go home and get some rest, Levi."

I nodded. I was on shift today, but nobody needed me to be out on the streets like this—least of all me.

"We'll meet back here again tomorrow morning and try this again."

Resolved and ready to get some space, I nodded my acquiescence and got the hell out of there.

My old truck started up on the first crank—the furthest thing from a given on days as cold as today—and I pulled out. Destination: unknown.

■

"Well, well, well, look what the toilet puked up."

I smiled at Jeremy and settled into the chair in front of his desk at the bank. He was a loan officer here, had been for a decade, and he was one of the most well-liked guys in town.

And he was a much better friend to me than I was to him.

"I'm sorry for last night."

"Yeah, well." He waved a hand. "My life would be too sedate without you anyway."

I shook my head and picked up the framed picture on his desk, turned it around, and rubbed my thumbs down the silver frame thoughtfully. His wife was laughing, her head thrown back as she looked up at him, their youngest baby on her hip, and he had their eldest daughter in the air, hands up and ready to catch her as she came down.

None of them gave even one fuck about the camera. Everything that was important to them was well within arm's reach.

"Your life is perfect," I said as I set the frame back in its place. And it was. He had it all figured out; what was important, what wasn't. I envied him with a poisonous intensity.

He smiled then, but his eyes, they stayed keen as they surveyed me closely. "So…what's up, Lee? What are you doing here?"

I smirked and steepled my fingers in front of my chest, pressing hard enough that a couple of them cracked. "I thought it was obvious. I'm apologizing."

His dark brown brows shifted closer together, and his mouth pursed. "Survey says that's bullshit. I've had to drag your drunk ass home more times than I can count, and I've never received such a royal showing. Something brought you here today other than clearing your conscience."

I did a quick once-over of his compact, muscled body, trying to calculate if I could take him. I knew he worked out five days a week, but I was a cop, for shit's sake. I was in superb physical condition.

Still, given the pint and a half of Jack still roiling around in my stomach, there would be better days to test it. I settled for verbal aggression instead.

"I could tell you what a fuckface you are for telling Nick about last night. Would that make you feel better? You know he tells Mona fucking everything. And once Mona knows, Old Red knows too."

He shrugged, completely unaffected.

The bastard. Why couldn't he ever take the bait like a normal fucking person?

Suddenly tired, I dropped the front and gave him the veneration he'd deserved from the beginning of this impromptu meeting. I was ninety-nine percent sure he'd spent time last night cleaning up my vomit. I was all kinds of an asshole for shit-stirring at all.

"Fine. I just… The chief gave me the day off—" He raised his eyebrows and sank back in his chair, hands at the back of his fresh-cut russet hair and elbows out. "Ordered it, really," I clarified with a hard swallow. "And I didn't want to go home."

He shook his head and rolled his eyes, but he pushed to his feet all the same. "Come on."

Forehead pinched, I followed his lead and got to my feet as he grabbed his jacket out of his closet and headed for the door. "We're going to breakfast," he told Karen, the twentysomething and very pretty receptionist at the front desk, when we passed her by. "I'll be back in an hour."

She smiled and nodded, briefly meeting my eyes with carnal interest. I considered it for half a second before tossing the idea out like garbage. She had too close of a connection to my friend and this town, and I only fucked strangers. I broke into a jog to catch up to Jeremy.

"Going to breakfast, huh?" I asked, slinging an arm around his shoulders.

He shook it off dramatically and shoved my shoulder. "Yep. And then you're going to go home and shower the fucking filth off of yourself and get some rest so you can be at my house at five thirty."

I barked a laugh. "And why's that?"

"Payback. The girls will be thrilled to have Uncle Levi as a babysitter tonight. I can hear their squeals now." My eyes narrowed playfully. "I'll make sure they have tons of new nail polish to try and all the latest Justin Bieber playing through the house when you get there."

I laughed, rubbed at my eyebrow with a very particular finger, and shook my head. "You're a cruel man, Jer."

But really, that sounded like exactly what I needed.

CHAPTER FIVE

Ivy

"**A**RE YOU SURE YOU'RE OKAY?" MY SISTER *AND* ASSISTANT, Camilla, asked for the fortieth time as I sat in the dark living room of Grace Murphy's little house with my phone to my ear. It was late—nearing midnight. I needed to go to bed, but my thoughts wouldn't slow and my mind wouldn't ease. After the tense encounter of this morning, the injury, and an endless stream of producers going over various details of the movie, I needed a little mindless chatter with my sister to take the day away.

I'd questioned early on whether involving family in my professional life was a good idea, but Camilla had turned out to be one of the best personal assistants in the business. Other celebrities were constantly trying to steal her away from me with fancy cars and promises of obscene money, and in the end, having a blood tie to keep her loyal to me wasn't such a bad thing.

"I'm fine. The doctor came and went three hours ago—" A point of contention, by the way, with many, many people. Mariah, Camilla, Jason, two of the producers—they'd wanted me to be seen immediately, but there was no way in hell I was going to let it interrupt my schedule for the day. I'd wrapped my hand loosely with gauze over the salve Glen had put on and agreed to a visit *after* I finished my meetings.

"The burns are only first degree, and I did the right thing by putting it under cold water. He wasn't thrilled that it'd been running from the tap, but he didn't see any signs of long-term damage. Plus, the cop who helped me put salve on it, right after getting it cooled made the active burning stop."

"Ooh," she cooed, my injury temporarily forgotten. "Hot cop tending to your wound. Sounds sexy."

I laughed and pulled the blankets covering me in my huddle on the couch up higher. Even with the heat turned up to seventy-five, I was fucking freezing. It probably didn't help that I'd naively packed silk camisoles and matching short-shorts for my pajamas.

"Not quite. Glen was very nice, but he's middle-aged and has a daughter in college."

I kept my mouth pointedly sealed about the cop who *was* hot—offensively so. He'd ruined any chances he had to star in my daydreams by being a colossal prick, and I didn't need Camilla hounding me about him.

"Bummer," she muttered glumly, and I laughed.

"I'm here to work. Not fall in love."

"That's the best time to fall in love!" she insisted. "When you're lost in your work and don't see it coming. Other celebrities do it all the time. Look at Channing and Jenna!"

I smiled and mindlessly picked at the quilt covering my knees. "I appreciate your enthusiasm, but I don't think this is like that."

"You never know—" Camilla started, but the flash of headlights through the front blinds caught my attention and distracted me.

"Who the hell is that?" I whispered without thinking.

Camilla picked up on the uncertainty in my voice immediately. "Where? What's going on? I thought you were at your house."

I jumped from the couch and ran to the front window, peeking through the blinds as discreetly as I could. The beams of the headlights blinded me, so I couldn't see much.

"I am," I murmured to Camilla. "Someone just pulled into the driveway."

The love-bitten version of my sister was gone in an instant, and in her place, my assistant Camilla took charge. "No one is supposed to know you're staying there, Ivy. Call the police."

I rolled my eyes and argued. "They're probably just turning around. I'm not calling the police."

"I thought the house was in the woods."

A shiver ran down my spine. "It is."

Oh my God. What if Mariah was right, and this is my stalker?

"Ivy, call the police," she ordered, just as the headlights shut off and the shadow of a man inside cut a menacing shape through the windshield.

"Oh, shit," I whispered, true panic taking hold for the first time since he'd pulled in. "Camilla, he just turned out the headlights."

"I'm calling the police!" she snapped before the line went dead.

My previously steady breathing devolved into pants as I sat there, frozen in the moment. After nearly a minute, he opened the door to the truck and moved to get out.

I jumped back from the window and, heart fluttering a hundred miles an hour, I backed up until my ass hit the couch.

Jesus Christ, what was I thinking, demanding that production secure Grace's house for me? Sure, stepping inside her world was the easiest, realest way to learn to be her, but she'd been murdered by a serial killer! She had lived in the middle of nowhere!

Yeah, and now you're here, in the middle of nowhere with a strange man outside…

Fuck, fuck, fuck!

Footsteps crunched in the gravel out front, and I had a fleeting thought that I might pass out.

I had no weapon, no means to protect myself, and I was in lingerie, for shit's sake.

Oh God. This is it. This is how it ends.

First rape, then murder.

The door creaked and cracked as the man on the other side forced it out of the frame and into the space of the small living room. My muscles locked, and everything inside me turned cold.

And my heart—it was beating so fast it felt like it wasn't beating at all.

The door shut, and his heavy shadow weighted the room. He was big and I was defenseless, but I had to try. "Stop right there!" I ordered on a nearly shrill scream.

He jumped at the sound of my voice, spewing curses left and right before finally finding the light switch next to the door.

At the sight of Levi Fox—*not* my stalker, thank God—standing there, five feet away, in the small living room of the house I'd rented for my time here, you could have knocked me over with a feather.

He looked good in all the ways he hadn't this morning, and it was painfully evident that this was his normal. But for all the tanned, warm skin and clear blue of his eyes, the shocked line of his mouth and the furrow of his brow stood out so starkly it was like all of his perfect features didn't exist.

"What in the *fuck* are you doing here?" he finally roared, his volume just shy of glass-shattering.

"I live here!" I yelled back. "What are *you* doing here?"

"This is Grace's house." His voice was raw and his edict unarguable. Something in the sandy rasp of his voice made me gentle mine.

"Her family rented it to the production company for me to stay in."

He shook his head almost violently, turning in a circle, and gave the wall next to the front door a look so vile, I was almost certain I'd be getting the opportunity to learn a thing or two about drywall repair.

He reeled it in, though, somehow, and turned back to look at me. His eyes were intense, and his appraisal of my body made me shake.

I wasn't decent, I knew that much. I was just a step up from pornographic, if I was honest. But sexy sleepwear was a guilty pleasure, and I clearly hadn't been expecting anyone out here.

He sounded strangled as he asked, "What are you wearing?"

Despite indisputable knowledge of how absurd I looked, I kept my answer simple. "Pajamas."

I got lost in the flare of his eyes for a second, maybe two, but ultimately, the clench of his fists was too obvious to ignore.

But what I found when I let myself look at them closely wasn't obvious at all.

"Is that *nail* polish?"

For half a second, he was self-conscious, but it didn't take him long to talk himself out of it. Apparently, the asshole inside of him was much better at battle than the insecure man.

"I was babysitting tonight. Not that that's any of your fucking business."

"It may not be *my* business, but I'm pretty sure CPS should be involved. Whoever leaves their kids with you can't be a good parent."

"Watch your fucking mouth," he snapped, his voice harsh to the point of scary. The old wood floor creaked with his weight as he leaned forward menacingly. "You don't know anything about me, and you sure as fuck don't know anything about Jeremy and Liza."

I was uncomfortable, a little scared of how badly he could hurt me if he was inclined, but as much as it looked like he might have wanted to, he didn't come any closer. I fought back with words and truth, the only way I knew how. I hoped they'd be enough to make him leave.

"I know you've shown up here, at my home for the moment, in the middle of the night, and accosted me."

"Accosted," he scoffed. His skin whitened at the roots of his hair, so rough was the hand he ran through it. "Sure is a fancy fucking word. No doubt something they taught you in Hollywood."

"What would you call it, then?" I shouted. "You showing up here in the middle of the night and treating me to this scene?"

His face was vehement, and his words weren't far behind. "Bad fucking luck. I didn't know you'd be here. Trust me, if I had, I'd have driven forty miles in the other direction."

It stung, his hatred. I felt the same way about him, and yet, somehow, I loathed that his opinion of me was so low. I guessed it was the people-pleasing part of me; it wanted acceptance no matter the people—even assholes.

Well, sexy assholes.

God, I hated my brain sometimes.

Lack of validation for that segment of my personality fueled another, though. The bitchy part.

My throat burned as I spat, "Dramatic, Officer Fox. Sounds like I'm not the only one with a penchant for Tinseltown."

"I don't need this bullshit," he grunted on an angry turn toward the door. As if *he* was the one inconvenienced by his unannounced arrival at my house.

I followed his retreat indignantly, bare feet smacking against the wood floor with every step, feeling emboldened to take a jab at him now that I knew he was leaving. "What's the matter, *Levi*? You can dish it out, but you can't take it?"

"A goddamn joke," he muttered as he ran his eyes over me once more and found only disgust. "Choosing *you* to play her. Red hair, green eyes, and a set of tits do *not* a Grace Murphy make."

"They chose me based on more than her appearance!"

His smile was lethal. "Keep telling yourself that, honey."

"What would you know about it?" I yelled, getting even more in his face. He planted his feet and bore my attack without moving.

He hadn't been in my audition. He hadn't cried the tears I had while letting Grace Murphy's last words haunt me. He didn't know *shit*.

His sapphire eyes moist with emotion, his voice was no more than a whisper. "More than you *ever* will."

The power in those five words rocked me.

Time jammed and slowed as I realized how off base my pride had taken me. How arrogant I'd been in my stubbornness.

Officer Fox.

For just a fraction of a moment, I was back in my audition, reading the scene where Grace lay on the floor, bleeding from her wounds and fighting for her life. There'd been a man there, tending to her, his face fuzzy through the ebbs in her consciousness. The script notes had said only one thing.

[The glint of his nameplate shines in her eyes. It reads "Officer Fox."]

Christ. He was the one. Grace, in a pool of agony and desperation, had died in this man's arms. *That* was why I'd recognized his name.

I'm such a fool.

There were a million stories and haunted memories in his eyes, and I didn't know why I hadn't seen it sooner. He'd known Grace well, better than I could even fathom in my limited time getting to know her through secondhand information. And like a vampire's vow, he'd just sworn to himself and me that I would never know the details of any of it.

CHAPTER SIX

Levi

WHY HAD ANYONE THOUGHT IVY STAYING IN GRACE'S HOUSE WAS okay?

Obviously, Hollywood had no goddamn problem trampling over her memory.

I wore pulsing temples like a symbol of my fury as I left Ivy behind, staring after me with the gentlest expression I'd ever seen her use.

I felt drunk from the confrontation, like my heart wasn't pumping enough blood and oxygen to my brain, and yet, she seemed composed. An eerie calm had overcome her in the last moments I'd allowed myself to stand there taking in the vision of her in light pink satin and lace scraps. And if I was honest, that scared me exponentially more than all of her pint-sized rage.

The familiar weather-stained wood of Grace's front porch under my feet, I moved as fast as I could toward my truck. But I didn't make it far before the ring of my cell phone in my pocket made me stop. I had half a mind to ignore it and concentrate on getting the fuck out of there, but the cop in me came awake and made me pull it out to look. The chief's information proclaimed he was the caller.

Without hesitation, I answered. "Chief?"

"Levi, thank fuck," he rumbled. "Dispatch got a call from Ivy Stone's sister, all the way in LA, panic in her blood about someone breaking in to Ivy's house. I'm on my way, but you're closer. She's at Grace's place."

Ah Christ.

My head dropped back, and my furious steps came to an abrupt stop. "I'm already here." The admission felt painful. I didn't have to elaborate for him to know why.

"Tell me you're not the shit-stain that was breaking in."

The bite of self-deprecation in my laugh tasted unpleasant. "That'd be me."

"Well, fuck. I hope she at least put a bullet in your shoulder."

Some days, I swore that'd make things easier. "No such luck, Red."

"Have you lost your goddamn mind? I mean, truly?"

"I didn't know she was staying here," I protested. There wasn't a snowball's chance in hell I would have shown up here if I'd known.

No, the truth was far more pathetic.

When the memories were strong and the regret became too much, coming here, to Grace's home, felt like the only way to get my head straight. Here, I could hear her telling me to stop being such a fuck-up. I could hear her telling me it was time to get over it. I could hear her telling me that a real man smiled when he wanted to yell.

Tonight, however, all I'd been able to hear was Ivy.

She had been screaming, though, so…

I took in a gulp of piercingly cold air and let it back out slowly. "In the future, that might be the kind of information I should have."

"Yeah, sure, Levi. Next time, I'll be sure to tell you in between you becoming blackout fucking drunk and getting in a fucking five-foot-three woman's face, that that same woman is staying at your old—"

"I get it," I interjected on a grouse.

"Do you really?" he asked. The disappointment of all my failures rang clearly in the words he didn't say. "I sure as hell hope so. Tomorrow morning, I want the asshole Levi gone and my reliable officer back. You understand me, son?"

For the four millionth time in two days, I gritted the words I'd been saying with ease for the last decade of my life. "Yes, sir." I wanted to make him proud, but feelings didn't turn off with a switch. I couldn't *make* myself be okay with all of this.

"Levi?" Ivy summoned from the porch. The sound of her calling my name ran through me like a current as the line went dead in my ear. My traitorous body went so far as to *like* it.

Immediately, every other fiber of me went on the defensive.

I swallowed hard around another knee-jerk reaction, one that would be hurtful and vile and all the things I'd just promised the chief I'd work on, and turned woodenly to face her.

"What, Ivy?" Her name was a snap, but all in all, I'd managed to prompt her for more information fairly normally.

"It's just…" She looked at me hard, trying to see beneath the surface, but my skin was thicker than that. With the life I'd lived, it had to be. "Is everything all right?"

I forced myself to examine her with new eyes—ones untainted by misery and remorse. Her wild hair was even more untamed than the two times I'd seen her previously, and her face was makeup free. Still, even without the aid of all that armor, her lashes were long and her skin nearly luminescent. And her body, clad in next to nothing, was the kind that made grown men into hormone-ridden adolescents.

I could play the part as though I saw none of it, but internally, in the sincere, lie-incapable section of my mind, I knew she was the stuff of legend.

It was no surprise this woman was followed and mimicked by millions—she was that beautiful.

I had to try a couple of times, the first attempt coming out garbled by the knot in my throat, but eventually, I got an explanation out. "Your sister. Apparently, she called the police." I pointed to myself with a hook of my thumb. "Police."

"Oh my God, Camilla!" Back into the house, she took off at a run.

I chewed at the inside of my lip, one of my anxious habits, and weighed my options. I could finish walking to my truck, climb in, and drive away—off to somewhere with a bottle or, at the very least, a bed. Or, I could follow her back into the home of a ghost that haunted me, just to say goodbye.

The smart part of me decided to leave almost immediately.

But the dumb part of me was much more persuasive these days.

I moved quickly to avoid rethinking and headed back up the steps and into the house. But this time, when I pushed open the door, I knocked.

She was pacing the living room, her hair completely hiding her face, but it flipped up and over in an impressive show as she heard my knuckles meet wood.

As she waved at me to come in, she talked. "No, no. I'm fine. It's fine. It was just a stupid mistake. I know him."

Her eyes flicked to mine briefly, and a roil of discomfort ran through my chest. I didn't like the idea of someone talking about me on the other end of that line, not being able to hear what they had to say.

"No, Jesus, would you stop? I told you it's not like that. I know him from work. He's one of the cops here."

She rolled her eyes but looked right at me, clearly repeating her sister for my benefit. "Yeah, Cam. I'm completely aware how ironic it is that we called the cops on a cop."

Caught off guard by the honest lilt of her self-effacement, I almost smiled.

Christ, I have to get out of here.

Ivy's eyes widened expressively as I waved my goodbye, but I didn't see them for long. I turned on my boot and went back out the door before I felt anything else. My manic moods had run the gamut today, and I was tired of living the extremes.

Besides, I'd be seeing her again soon—first thing tomorrow morning.

CHAPTER SEVEN

Ivy

MONA'S FACE DID NOTHING TO DISGUISE HER FEELINGS ABOUT MY outfit as I stepped into the Cold Montana Police Department for the second day in a row.

I'd had all sorts of grandiose visions about the outfits I should be wearing, but planning didn't always translate into ease of execution.

"I know. Trust me, I know. I ordered some plain jeans off of Amazon yesterday as soon as I left the station, but they won't be here until tomorrow. I can't believe you don't have same-day delivery. And the closest mall is two hours away!"

White silk, my blouse billowed around my midsection with a flirtatious drape where I'd tucked the front of it into my rhinestone-encrusted jeans. They just had tiny clusters every so often, but they weren't the makings of a simple outfit. And, on top of it all, the same Zac Veeson coat. My brown suede ankle booties weren't exactly backcountry, but the flat sole was at least practical.

Mona's answering smile was downright comical. Overexaggerated and toothy in the middle, she was basking in my misery. "Welcome to Montana."

The phone trilled its demand to be answered, and she held up one unmanicured finger toward me. Just as I nodded, a body-numbing wind rolled up my spine. The door had evidently opened behind me.

My smile bright and welcoming, I turned to greet the chief for the second morning in a row. Only, instead of wily eyebrows and an untucked shirt, I found Levi, clothed in a crisp, pressed uniform and shiny black shoes. He looked as handsome as the time I'd first laid eyes on him—if not better.

His eyes were pointed at my mouth, a tiny wrinkle forming in the skin between his eyebrows.

I spoke quickly even as my smile dimmed, trying to head off the confrontation before it came to pass. "Good morning, Levi."

"Ivy." His answer was a grunt. Nearly monosyllabic. But at least he wasn't calling me a stuck-up bitch.

I struggled to find conversation for the first time in my life. The door, the ceiling, the floor, and my shoes—all of it became complex and inspection-worthy.

Oh, look, it's my shoes. The same shoes I put on this morning. Wow, let's keep looking at them for no apparent reason at all. Maybe they'll get interesting soon...

I wasn't accustomed to not knowing what to say. Normally, I could chat my ass off, ask interesting and insightful questions, and make people feel completely comfortable. But, apparently, when it came to Levi Fox, I only knew what to say when I was yelling.

Mona, bless her, interrupted our silent evasion. "Got a callout, Levi. It's Joe Morris. He's supposedly got a squatter on the property, and his wife says he just came in and got his shotgun."

"Fucking hell," Levi muttered with a shake of his head. "On it." He didn't acknowledge me at all before turning and shoving back out the door, moving to his cruiser in the back lot at a brisk clip.

Without even thinking, I went after him.

"Levi!" I yelled as he rounded the corner of the building. He didn't slow, so I sped up. Salty, slushy gravel crunching under my boots, I ran as fast as I could without busting my ass.

He had the driver's door open and was dropping into the seat when I finally caught up.

"Levi! Wait!"

"I gotta go, Ivy," he said, his patience waning. "The man's waving a shotgun around if you didn't hear. We'll have our meeting when I get back."

I ignored his insinuation and used all of the breath I had left after the jog to demand, "Take me with you."

His mouth turned down at the corners. "Fuck no."

"Please," I begged desperately, my hands shaking as I clasped them in front of me.

I wasn't sure whether to blame it on the cold or the thirst for experience.

This—riding along to a real-life scenario—was exactly what I needed. I could have all the meetings in the world with as many police officers as would give me their time, but I needed to be out there in the field.

I needed to feel real fear and test out my ability to make split-second decisions. Only then would I be able to understand what Grace had gone through.

"I need this. I don't need the stupid meeting where we talk and stare at each other uncomfortably for an hour. I *need* to know what it's *really* like out there."

He held my beseeching gaze for what felt like forever.

When the suspense finally ended, his grunt seemed mined from the deepest recesses of his self-control. "Get in. Quickly."

I booked. Feet pounding, arms churning, I rounded the car as fast as my lungs would allow. If I thought I could have pulled it off, I would have jumped up and slid across the hood like an action hero.

I barely had my ass in the seat, my door not fully closed, when Levi slammed his foot on the gas, put a hand to my headrest, and backed up on a spray of gravel. Wisely, I didn't bother to try to reach for the door as it swung out of my hand, and though it was fighting valiantly to be released, managed to keep my scream inside my throat.

The door situation righted itself, thankfully shutting closed as he pulled the shifter into drive and slammed his foot onto the gas again.

I glanced over cautiously, cataloging the focus on his face for future reference.

"So…uh…do you get calls like this a lot?"

"People take their property pretty seriously around here, Ivy. If you weren't an out-of-towner, I would have spent all last night fishing buckshot out of my skin."

The corner of his mouth lifted upward for the first time since he'd caught me in a lie, and I thought I might faint. Hand to God, he was the living, breathing, modern-day version of Adonis.

I had to ignore it.

A couple of days in and we'd been nothing but two left feet, tripping over one another so much we had no option but to drag the other down in a bid to survive.

Finally, I felt like I'd gotten some of my coordination back. Sure, he was making fun of me now, but I would take it. Anything that kept us from being at each other's throats and got in the way of my being able to learn what I needed to about Grace Murphy.

And thinking he was *attractive*—or God forbid letting that fascination grow into *wanting* him—would undoubtedly take us right back down the spiral to hell.

He reached forward and flicked on the lights and siren with a sinewy, veined arm, and then took the first right at an alarming speed. When he came to the next intersection, a left was our fate.

He didn't look to anything to guide him, and another question popped into my head. "I take it you know where Joe Morris lives?" Mona hadn't given him an address or anything.

He nodded, the strong line of his jaw flexing with the motion. "I know where everyone lives in Cold."

"Wow." That seemed like a lot of information to keep up with, but he was already shaking his head without my even having to say anything to that effect.

"I've lived here all my life. Been a cop here for a decade. And there's not a whole lot of turnover. Most of these people have lived on the property they live on now longer than I've been alive."

People didn't move? In LA, people were looking for bigger and better places on what seemed like a weekly basis. The idea that all of these people could be happy in the same place for the span of their entire life fascinated me—especially given the reason I was here in the first place.

And he'd been a cop for a decade? Wow. That meant he had to be in his thirties—depending on what he'd done for school, maybe even thirty-five. I wasn't sure he'd react kindly to a question about his age, though, so I kept my ponderings to myself.

"Nobody took off when the Cold-Hearted Killer was here? What about after?"

"Talking time is over," Levi announced as my body pushed into the door with the force of our turn into Joe Morris's driveway. I wasn't an expert in the town, I didn't know where everyone lived, but the guy standing out in the front pasture with a shotgun pointed directly at another guy was a dead giveaway. "Stay in the car," he ordered as we slid to a dramatic stop and the gear shifter slipped easily into park.

He didn't give me time to agree or disagree. He moved so quickly it seemed like one second he was next to me, and the following, he was walking straight at the guy with the gun.

I strained my ears to hear what they were saying from inside the car, but the thing may as well have been a well-constructed voice-over booth. I couldn't hear a damn thing.

Unacceptable.

First, in an attempt to follow orders, I searched the door panel for a button to put the window down. I found it, but when I pressed the button, it didn't do anything. The car was still running; there hadn't been enough time to shut it off, so I had to assume police cars came equipped with child locks on steroids for any and all controls not within the cabin of the driver himself.

Dejected, I focused back out the windshield, on Levi's back—right as Joe Morris took the gun he had pointed at the squatter and turned it on Levi.

Something overcame me, boiling deep from the pit of my stomach and turning my throat raw. I didn't hesitate, and I most certainly didn't think.

Because if I had, I was pretty sure I wouldn't have ended up with the gun pointed at *me*, wind whipping a sting into my nose as I yelled, "Stop!"

Just a minute ago, I'd been in the warmth of Levi's police car, struggling to hear, and now, I was out in the cold, staring down the barrel of a shotgun with an angry Levi at my back. One positive, though—I could hear just fine.

"Ivy!" Levi growled. "Have you lost your goddamn mind?"

It wasn't a ridiculous question. Fear and adrenaline pounded through my arms, the tips of my fingers tingling with the intensity, and for the first time in my life, I questioned whether my lack of impulse control was a bad thing. Up until this point, all of my rash decisions had only led to moments that changed my life for the better.

But this one had the potential to affect my life in a whole other way—by ending it.

CHAPTER EIGHT

Levi

OUT TO THE SIDE LIKE A FLAG, IVY'S HAIR WHIPPED IN THE WIND so violently it looked like it'd take her head with it. I, perversely, stood frozen in place as everything in my past collided with the present.

"Stop!" she yelled, the sound of her voice like a bullet in the open Montana air. It cracked through the silence and hit me in the chest hard enough that I came back to life.

"Ivy!" I yelled. Her name sounded rough in the unforgiving winter air, like it didn't go with all the leftover snow and tranquility. "Have you lost your goddamn mind?"

Her ridiculous outfit was like a comedian in the middle of a full-on drama and reminded me that I didn't know her mind at all. For as much as she looked like a woman I'd known for most of my life, a woman she was supposed to be learning to embody, her mind was something entirely different.

Maybe this was normal behavior for her. Maybe she took huge risks and led with her heart. Maybe she didn't know how to think through a situation at all.

"Hi," she said to Joe Morris, extending a hand out for him to shake like there wasn't a gun pointed at her pretty face. "I'm Ivy Stone."

Time slowed as I stepped forward. I moved with the speed of a turtle, afraid anything faster might startle Joe into pulling the trigger.

"Ivy," I called again, but this attempt was gentler.

Neither she nor Joe was listening.

But the gun came down—one inch, two, until the barrel was finally pointing toward the lifeless ground.

"Ivy Stone?" Joe mused, rolling the hard planes of her name around on his tongue. "My wife talks about your movies all the time. What in Sam Hill are you doin' here?"

"Making a movie," she replied with a simple smile.

Joe looked around behind us, the squatter long forgotten as he took off at a run down the lane and out into the wilderness. I had a feeling I'd be getting another call about him, from someone else, in a couple of days. "You got a film crew here now?"

But I was done. I couldn't stand here and listen to this shit for even a second longer. My fuse had been lit, was burning at an alarming rate, and it would be a hell of a lot better for all involved if it didn't blow here.

"Joe," I cut in. "Next time you have a problem, call the police instead of going for your gun."

I couldn't tell you his response because I didn't wait for it. I grabbed Ivy by the elbow and dragged her back to the car, her little legs churning at double speed to keep up. When we got to the hood, I let her go with a small but gentle shove, ordering, "Get in the fucking car. Now."

Thankfully, telling her to get in went over better than telling her not to get out. She moved quickly to jump in the passenger seat and shut her door, and I took a full breath for the first time since she'd stepped in front of me and into the line of fire.

If it hadn't been for the cutesy wave she'd given Joe through the windshield as I put the car in reverse and pressed my foot to the gas, I might have cooled down.

Now, my fire was raging, and there wasn't a chance in hell of putting it out anytime soon.

"You're insane!" I shouted into the confined space. Ivy winced. The volume was enough to bust your eardrums, I knew, but I had absolutely no control over it. None. It had been abandoned, a mile of bad road back in the other direction. "A fucking certifiable lunatic! I should turn you over my knee."

Foot nearly to the floor, I was driving way too fast, but I needed her out of the car. I needed to make it back to the station and put as much distance between us as possible before I lost my mind. I felt like my younger self, wild and violent and rebellious. I didn't want to act like the cop I'd grown into with her here. I *couldn't*. She flipped some sort of switch, and until she wasn't around anymore, I couldn't flip it back.

"Levi—"

I refused to let her speak.

"That's it. No more. I thought I could be nice and try to take you along. Give you a goddamn chance, but *no more*," I seethed, fear and worry and history and *awful fucking memories* all swirling in my mind to create rage. "You've obviously got a death wish, and I'm not about to cart you around, giving you chances to make it happen!"

"Oh, come on. This wasn't about some hedonistic suicide attempt. He had a gun pointed at you!"

"Yeah, I know. It's happened more than once, and it'll happen again. But I've been trained for it! Not sure if you remember, but I'm the actual cop out of the two of us."

"I'm the one who defused the situation," she argued stubbornly.

God, the idea of taking her over my knee and spanking her little ass grew more desirable by the second.

"Joe Morris had as much of a chance of shooting me as you have at riding along with me ever again. He knew my grandfather. He held me as a baby. Information I took into account when I got out of the car and walked right at him. You…" I shook my head. "I don't know what in the hell *you* were thinking!"

"I was thinking—"

"You weren't thinking at all," I interrupted. "Not one fucking thing!"

Finally—fucking finally—I turned into the parking lot of the station, pulled into a spot, and shut off the engine. I thought I'd jump right out, put the distance between us immediately, but the pull to yell at her was still too strong.

"Of all the stupid, self-destructive things you could—"

There was no notice. No time to prepare. Lungs fully engaged and voice gruff with emotion, I was halfway through my latest diatribe when she leaned forward and slammed her lips to mine.

Flesh to flesh, she inhaled, taking in my scent and replacing it with the fruity medley of her own, and I had to work to keep breathing. Her lips were sweet, and her presence was…*overwhelming*.

God, she tastes good.

I kicked feverishly for the surface as every hot touch of her mouth pulled me under, but the taste of her tongue was too sweet and the electricity running through my body too real.

Her lips were supple and insistent, and her tongue worked at mine intimately. It was knowing and direct, and God, it was like we'd kissed a million times in a million lives before this one.

When I finally found the will to break it off, I was half hard and angrier than ever. Angry that she'd done it. Angry that she'd caught me off guard. *Furious* that I couldn't convince myself not to like it.

"What the *fuck* are you doing?"

Her green eyes were wide, off-kilter in a way I suspected my own mirrored. But regardless of the shock, her reply was unrepentant. "I had to do something to shut you up. And since you have a gun on your hip, kissing you seemed like a better option than any form of physical violence."

CHAPTER NINE

Ivy

Nerves fried already, I nearly came out of my skin as Levi slammed his door with a crack and stalked toward the station.

Did I really just kiss him?

Sweet merciful shotgun, I was so fucking mortified, I daydreamed briefly about going back to Joe Morris's land and having him put me out of my misery.

The decision to kiss Levi had been so sudden it was nonexistent, and looking back, I couldn't even pinpoint it as a moment in time. I'd been sitting there, trying to get a word in edgewise as he yelled and berated and called my intelligence into question again and again. His features had been severe and intense, but I remembered thinking they were so obviously *involved*.

My well-being and the threat to it—that was what had him hysterical.

And, God, even madder than fire, he'd looked so good.

The next thing I knew, I was on him like white on rice.

I could still feel the tingle of his lips on mine, the recklessness with which he'd kissed me back branded on my body like a physical mark. I didn't even think he'd known he was doing it, maybe still didn't know that he had, but Levi Fox, one of the biggest assholes I'd ever met, had just given me the *best* kiss of my *life*.

As a result, I suspected he hated me even more. My response? The opposite.

To say I was intrigued by him would have been the understatement of the century.

For some inexplicable reason, I felt drawn to Levi like a moth to a flame.

How in the hell was I supposed to deal with that?

■

Flurries floated mindlessly to the ground outside the window of Grace's house as Boyce Williams, producer on *Cold*, droned on from his spot at the kitchen table. The sun was setting over the tops of the still lush evergreens on the property, and the evening appeal of a good stiff drink had never looked better.

I was trying hard to listen to every word and detail as he shuffled through the beginning of the script and a few small changes they'd had the screenwriter make, but I was too lost in the chaos of my thoughts.

They were the exact opposite of the steady calm snow outside, and they heated my cheeks to a ruby shine.

I'd been the one to kiss Levi Fox.

But, Jee-zus, he'd wrecked me.

So much so I couldn't fucking concentrate.

"…So, in the opening scene, when Grace was in the station alone, weaving through file after file of information on the victims, we're going to have Levi Fox be there with her instead."

My head jerked up at the sound of his name.

"Levi Fox?"

Boyce nodded as though I'd been following along all this time. "Yeah. The research team thinks highlighting a male and female lead will make the film resonate with more male viewers."

I rolled my eyes. *Of course,* they thought people would care more about the movie if it wasn't all about a woman.

"Plus, adding a romance aspect to the film will appeal to more viewers in general."

"A *romance* aspect?" I questioned. That definitely hadn't been a part of the original screenplay.

Grace's determination, her strength, her character, her sacrifice? Yes.

But romance? *No.*

"Yes, between Grace and Levi."

"But I thought the point was to keep it as close to factual as possible…"

Grace and Levi had been coworkers. Two cops who were striving to solve an important case in a small town. A case that involved a serial killer.

What in the fuck did romance have to do with that?

Boyce tilted his head, each degree of the cocked angle taking his condescension to a douchier level. "It's *based* on a true story, Ivy. But it's not a fucking documentary. The goal is to make money."

Pain pricked as I clamped down on my tongue. It was gearing up to run away, I could feel it, and the last thing I needed to do was lose my job. If I blew this, it'd be the top of an ugly downward spiral to nothingness. But beyond that, I'd be doing Grace Murphy a huge disservice. I knew for a fact that no other Hollywood diva they could bring up here would care even one iota as much as I did about getting her right.

Boyce sighed. "Just go over the changes with a fine-tooth comb. Johnny

Atkins will be up here in a week and a half to start filming, and the two of you will need to be on the same page."

I nodded. I knew all about the director, Hugo Roman, and his unyielding demands for instant chemistry. I hadn't worked with him before, but tales ran wide of his propensity to shoot love scenes *first*, just to make sure the male and female lead had the heat necessary to take his film to the top of the box office.

I attempted to picture Johnny Atkins as I thumbed through the script long after Boyce left me to my solitude. I endeavored to see his smile when Grace exchanged jokes with him, his heavy scowl when she did something he didn't like, and his long lash-rimmed eyes when his stare scrutinized Grace's choices.

I *tried*.

The only problem was that I knew Levi Fox—he was complicated and layered and hotter than any man I'd ever laid eyes on, in person or otherwise.

And I wasn't sure that Johnny Atkins's version, no matter what he did, would ever be able to live up to the real one.

■

Laughter rang out in the open space around Ruby Jane's as I slammed the door shut on my rental and pulled the front of my coat tighter around my body. The red neon in the apostrophe was dimmer than the rest of the sign, and the brown building looked worn from years of use. As the only watering hole in Cold, Montana, though, I suspected the lack of curb appeal did nothing to diminish a steady flow of patrons.

I had on my fancy jeans and a lavender cashmere sweater, but the day of activity in the snow had done a number on my brown suede ankle booties. They had stains and irreversible damage that would make any fashionista cry. I, perversely, now had hopes that they would bring my outfit down a couple of notches, to a level that would blend.

I wanted a drink and I wanted the hum of public noise, but I wasn't in the mood to be noticed. The irony was almost too rich—an up-and-coming Hollywood actress trying to *avoid* attention.

Trust me, no matter what they say publicly, it's usually the other way around.

Cold, brass door handle in both hands, I had to lean all of my body weight into the door to get it open. That should have tipped me off.

But I was too busy thinking about what I'd order to heed any warning born of common sense.

Just barely in the door, I surveyed the room as I let the door fall closed behind me. But the suction of the indoors and the wind from outside were too strong and my body too slight, and before I knew it, I was careening forward in a film-worthy fall that ended on my hands and knees thanks to a solid wood slap in the ass.

Grit from people's shoes and undissolved ice salt stung sharply in the palms of my hands, purple bruise blood pooled at my knees, and, perhaps above all, humiliation ached in the pit of my stomach.

Silence descended as bar-goers noticed my less than graceful entrance one by one. Head down beneath my protective curtain of hair, I stayed there, waiting for absolution to swallow me whole.

Square-toed boots stopped just short of my fingertips, and the dagger to my pride sank a little deeper. Up the denim, my gaze began its march to find the owner, and when it did, I knew I had my answer.

Just like Rose, lonely and freezing in the middle of the cold Atlantic as the *Titanic* went down, it didn't matter how much I prayed.

For me, tonight, absolution would never come—only a conundrum named Levi Fox staring down at me.

CHAPTER TEN

Levi

CHEEKS THE COLOR OF HER HAIR, IVY LOOKED UP AT ME FROM HER hands and knees. Her eyes were misty with aches and embarrassment as I reached down with both hands and lifted from under her armpits. I'd noticed how small she was, but I still wasn't prepared for her to be so featherlight.

When she'd opened the door and stepped inside, white-hot annoyance had made the surface of my skin tingle. I didn't want her to be here. I liked to drink alone, and I did it with the purpose of going numb. Ivy, for all she was, was the last thing in my life that would aid in my bid for apathy.

Exhibit A: I'd been out of my seat as soon as she hit the floor.

"You all right?"

She nodded and tucked her chin, the prospect of meeting my eyes too much in the fresh hell of public mortification.

"I'm fine."

I nodded back above her head in an effort to give her the benefit of secrecy in her true feelings, but avoiding her eyes meant noticing others, and believe you me, the eyes of the town were upon us.

"Come on," I ordered thickly, trying not to let the invasion of privacy turn me callous. I knew my trigger had only a breadth of forgiveness these days, and all that communal inspection was hell on its sensitivity. "Let's go."

"Where?" she asked, her vivid green eyes meeting mine for the first time.

The question caught me off guard. *Surely, she wants to leave, right?* She'd just fallen to her knees in one of the most attended places in all of Cold. There wasn't a chance in Hades she'd be able to do anything for the rest of the night without being watched, and I'd stupidly cared enough about her well-being to connect us via being the first person to run to her aid *and* support her with my own hands. She *had* to go.

"To your car. I'll help you."

Her eyebrows drew together a half an inch and stood up in the center, and the slow shake of her head swirled a curl of dizziness through my mind. "I'm not leaving."

"Ivy," I nearly growled, the determination in her voice making mine get heated. "Come on. I'll walk you to your car."

"I'm *not* leaving."

"Ivy. Turn the fuck around."

"I'm not leaving!" she yelled. Time contracted on that one moment, and any-fucking-body who'd been oblivious to our meeting of the minds before wasn't anymore.

My hands left her arms quickly—as if they burned.

"Fine," I gritted. "Suit yourself."

Our separation was bitter, and the crickets chirped almost violently as we both walked over to the bar—me, back to my seat, and her to the farthest stool at the other end.

Lou had already filled my glass when I returned, so I picked it up with a shaking hand and downed it. The silky warmth that coated my throat in its wake made it easier to sit down and blind myself to the rest of it.

I didn't see her hair or her scowl or her haunting green eyes, and I couldn't hear the whispers. I didn't care what she was doing or who she was with or if she even stayed there after that. It was just me and my glass, and I took a trip to oblivion.

Three hours and seven glasses of whiskey later, a ghost from my past found my arm and set out to mend the hurt from earlier.

"Levi?" Grace asked me softly, her voice a little different than normal, but still pretty.

I squinted, trying to find enough focus to make out her perfect features, but all I could manage was a blurry painting of green, peach, and red.

"Grace," I hummed with a smile. "Iss good to see you."

The pink of her mouth changed shape, flattening out at the corners, and I reached up with a thumb to try to smooth it.

"It's good to see you too, Levi."

"Where you been? You get mad at me or somefin?" Deep into the recesses of my brain that hadn't let alcohol drown out logic, I knew it didn't add up. But I ignored the truth. It was easier that way. *Simple, easy. Yeah. That sounds so nice.*

The big blob of her hair shook back and forth, and her answer was a whisper. "No."

"Thas good," I remarked, followed by a "Whoa." She had a shoulder under my arm and was lifting me off my stool before I could protest. She'd always been a stout little thing. "You're strong, you know that?" I muttered. "So strong."

"I didn't really," she said weirdly. "But I'm starting to get it now."

My brain ached, like my skull was abrasive and too tight around the membrane, and I blinked to open my eyes, but the light stabbed at me like a knife.

What in God's hell had I done last night?

Rebelling against the pain, I forced my eyes open, expecting to see Jeremy's couch or the sheets of my own bed courtesy of him. Anytime I got drunk, he was the one to deal with it. He didn't have a signed contract or anything, but his number was the lucky one Lou could reliably find on his speed dial.

What I found instead made me sit up entirely too fast. Vomit threatened, and my eyes burned.

Thankfully, a trash can sat next to the plaid couch, a fresh bag lining the inside. I heaved and purged, voiding myself of the rotten alcohol in no more than thirty seconds.

A bottle of water on the coffee table quenched the cottony dryness of my tongue and rinsed out everything putrid.

Things were looking up.

Relief was sweet but brief as I realized with renewed clarity where I was.

The banana yellow curtains and soft cream walls. The painted butterfly on the back of the front door and the furry gray pillow behind my back.

This was Grace's living room.

Ivy's living room.

Jesus Christ.

I had to get out of there.

Listening intently for signs of a woman awake, I tied up the now disgusting trash bag beside the couch with plans to dispose of it in one of the outside bins, pulled on my boots at the foot of the couch, and grabbed my jacket from where it'd been draped over the back.

The air was still and the morning silent—thank God—so I moved to the door on the tips of my toes, pausing for only a moment, hand on the knob, my gaze no more than a passing glance.

Come hell or high water, I had to find a way to put both of the women in this house behind me.

CHAPTER ELEVEN

Ivy

The frigid Montana wind whipped at my face as I stood my ground near Levi's cruiser, my back resting against the closed trunk. He walked toward me, his boots crunching in the gravel of the parking lot with each step. When our eyes met, his mouth turned into a scowl.

"This is starting to get old, Ivy," he said as he passed me and moved toward the driver's-side door.

Instantly, I smarted. The day after I'd spent three and a half hours watching him turn himself into a drunken shell of a human being, hauled him to my car, dragged him into my house, and taken care of his basic needs as he'd passed out, I'd been understanding. The memory of his eerie conversation with me as Grace was still fresh in my mind and heart, and I knew I had to give him some time.

But it'd been seven fucking days since then, and enough was finally enough. Something had to give, and evidently, Levi Fox was only equipped to take.

He wasn't the only one who'd lost Grace, but he was the only one who couldn't seem to stop blaming me for it. Over the last week, I'd gotten a call from Grace's mother, Mary, welcoming me to town, and a series of sweet text messages from her grandpa Sam that gave me hope. They wanted me here. They were kind and open, and they understood I would do my best to give Grace the closure she deserved.

Why couldn't Levi see that?

"You ignoring me is getting old. We have to work together. Grace deserves a well-developed depiction of her character, and the two of us are going to have to talk in order to make that happen. Apparently, only one of us can see that."

He pulled up short, spun on his heel, and got directly in my face. The downturn of his mouth was severe, and the light in his eyes was chilling. "There's something you need to understand right fucking now." His voice dropped, lower, deeper, *harsher,* and I fought the urge to grimace. "I don't owe you anything, and you don't know a *goddamn* thing about me or Grace or what I care about."

I found the mark in the sand and immediately jumped back a step. The goal of showing up here every day, at the police station, wasn't to fight. I'd clearly let my mouth get ahead of me. "I'm…I'm sorry. You're right. That was completely out of line."

He stared at me for a long moment, his eyes practically burning me with rage.

"I'm really sorry, Levi," I apologized again. "I just want—"

"I don't care about what you want," he cut me off. "If it were up to me, this film would *not* be happening, and you sure as fuck wouldn't be here."

Slack-jawed and completely shocked, I watched as he stalked away from me, his black boots pounding against the gravel until he reached the driver's door and hopped in.

I moved away from his cruiser, knowing I'd more than lost today's battle and a little fearful he'd run me over if he had to, and headed toward the warmth of the station to fight off the cold.

stone

The engine of his cruiser revved to life behind me, and moments later, he was gone.

Good Lord, exhaustion was just around the corner if he kept it up with the anger and irritation. It seemed like we couldn't go one fucking round without someone aiming for a knockout.

Don't get me wrong, I understood the fragility of the situation. I wasn't oblivious to the fact that Grace had been important to him. She was his partner. Someone he had grown up with. And from what I'd gathered, a very close friend.

But the ire of his wrath felt unwarranted and directed solely at me.

I was merely asking him to tell me more about her. Not because I was selfish or nosy or wanted to railroad through territory I knew was very sensitive, but because I wanted to make sure when I got in front of the camera, I was doing Grace justice.

To me, this film wasn't just about the money. It was about a woman who had the strength to stop a sociopath. A man who, had he not been stopped, would've no doubt taken more lives.

But fuck, Levi Fox sure was making it hard.

I looked around the otherwise quiet station until my gaze caught sight of Officer Glen, dressed head to toe in his Cold Police uniform and filling a small Styrofoam cup with coffee. With thick fingers and unassuming eyes, he added two packets of sugar and one small creamer to his brew before snapping it closed with a plastic lid. By the time he'd started to head for the door, I made my move.

"Hey, Glen," I greeted, sidling up to him with a soft smile. "Mind if I ride with you today?"

"Uh…" He stopped in his tracks, and the wrinkles around his gray eyes crinkled at the corners as he looked down at me. "The chief put you with Levi…" he said, but it was more of a question than a statement.

"Well, it looks like I'll be riding with you now."

It still wasn't what I *really* needed to happen, but surely Officer Glen Chase had useful information about Grace. He'd worked with her. He was active when the Cold-Hearted Killer situation had gone down.

"Nuh-uh." He shook his head and raised both hands in the air like I was holding him hostage. Coffee sloshed out of the small hole in the lid of his cup, and droplets spattered onto the worn tile floor. "I'm not getting in the middle of this."

"What?" I questioned, acting completely confused. "Trust me, Glen, there isn't anything to get in the middle of. This is simply an adjustment of schedule. I'm sure the chief won't mind."

"You're a good actress, Ivy Stone," he said, and an amused chuckle escaped his lips. "But it's not the chief I'm worried about."

"What is that supposed to mean?"

"We both know exactly what that means," he added, and without giving me any more time to plead my case, he strode out the door with his gun securely in its holster, coffee in his right hand, and an amused smile still etched across his lips.

Dammit. I really thought it would've worked…

I hitched my hip against one of the empty desks inside the station and weighed out my options. It was a remarkably quick process because there were none.

Levi had made it pretty damn clear he wanted nothing to do with me. Glen didn't want to get in the middle of whatever he felt he would be getting in the middle of. And I was pretty sure there weren't any Cold cops left in the station to help me.

Well, there is one…

Dane Marx. I'd learned pretty quickly everyone called him "the rookie," and from what I'd seen so far, he lived up to the nickname. Twenty-four, fresh out of the police academy, and rarely given the opportunity to go on the "serious" police calls, to say he was still learning the ropes would've been an understatement.

But he *was* working today, and although I wasn't sure if he even knew Grace, I was certain he could provide me with some insight into Levi. And with blond hair, bright green eyes, and a nearly constant boyish grin, he was also *real* easy on the eyes.

But will he let me ride along?

There was only one way to find out.

By the time I reached his desk, he was standing up from his chair and pulling his jacket over his arms.

"There you are," I said. Immediately, his eyes met mine and his brow furrowed. He looked over his shoulder and then back at me before finally asking, "Are you talking to me?"

I almost laughed. Besides Mona and a few stragglers who worked on the administrative end, we were practically the only two in the station.

"Of course I'm talking to you, silly." I wasn't proud of it, but I flashed him my movie-star smile in a shameless attempt to butter him up. "Chief Pulse instructed me to ride along with you today."

"With me?"

Cute and maybe a little slow on the uptake sometimes.

"Yep." I nodded.

"But I thought Levi was—"

"Is it time to head out?" I chimed in before he asked me a question that would require another lie. Even though acting could be misconstrued as a form of lying, I wasn't a fan of *actual* lying, especially to handsome, unsuspecting twenty-four-year-olds with boy-next-door smiles.

Dane looked at me closely for a quiet moment, but to my surprise, no forms of questioning or police interrogation left his lips. Like a true rookie, he took my word as Gospel.

"Well, okay then," he said, and two small dimples formed in his cheeks. "I'd be honored to have you ride along with me, Ms. Stone."

"Oh God," I muttered on a laugh. "No need to be so formal. Please, call me Ivy."

"Okay, *Ivy*," he said and flashed that familiar boyish grin once more. I had a feeling most women had a hard time saying no to it. "Let's go."

We were out the door and inside his cruiser a few minutes later. With a turn of a key, the engine roared to life and we were off, heading out of the parking lot and roaming the currently action-less city streets of Cold.

There wasn't much to see, or do, for that matter, but I tried to make the best of it by mentally calculating how to steer a conversation toward Levi without making it too obvious.

A few minutes into our drive, he glanced toward me out of his periphery, and the biggest smile consumed his face. "I can't believe I'm driving famous Ivy Stone around Cold, Montana in my cruiser today." He looked at me once more before gently flexing his fingers against the leather of the steering wheel. "I am one lucky son of a bitch."

"No way." I waggled my index finger at him. "I'm the lucky one today."

He chuckled, and his cheeks flushed a little at my words. "Drop-dead gorgeous and a sweet-talker, you're a dangerous woman, Ivy."

God, he was adorable. And, if I was being honest, pretty damn hot.

Not only did he have that boy-next-door look, but underneath his police uniform, it appeared he also had a pretty damn good body.

I knew for a fact that I wasn't the only one inside this small town who had come to that conclusion, though. Dane Marx was quite the ladies' man. The last and only time I was at Ruby Jane's, I'd managed to catch a glimpse of him in all of his smooth-talking, charming glory.

"Like you should talk. I've seen you in action before, you know."

"In action?"

"Uh-huh." I grinned. "Ruby Jane's about a week ago. You were sitting near the pool tables in the back surrounded by a bunch of women who were batting their eyelashes and giggling at anything and everything you said."

A soft chuckle left his full lips. "I have no idea what you're talking about."

Liar. Liar. Pants on fire.

It was my turn to laugh. "Unless you've got a doppelgänger in this small town, you know exactly what I'm talking about."

My mind, the devious fucking thing, decided now was a good time to compare the way the women of Cold responded to Dane versus Levi.

Dane was charming, always smiling, and the women who had flocked around him at the bar had looked like they were at ease in his presence, nothing more on their agenda than laughing and having a good time.

Levi Fox was a whole different animal.

Brooding and moody with a face that gave nothing away, he was an enigma. But, God, I'd seen the way the women at Ruby Jane's had looked at him with erotic interest. It was like he was the James Dean to their quest to find a bad boy to take to bed.

Even the ones who'd been chatting up Dane couldn't stop themselves from glancing in Levi's direction. While he'd drunk himself into a stupor, the interest and intrigue shining within their eyes had only grown. A tortured man held a power over the part of a woman that wanted to heal hurts—the innate drive to nurture.

Yeah, and you're no different...

I shook off that thought and focused back on Dane. He smirked softly as he glanced at me out of the corner of his eyes.

"It was just a few friends," he said, referring to the very women who'd been swooning over him.

"A few friends who all happened to be of the female variety."

"Mere coincidence." He chuckled softly again.

"Sure, it was."

He smirked and shrugged his shoulders, but he kept his eyes firmly on the road this time.

"So, tell me, Officer Marx, how long have you been charming the ladies in Cold, Montana?"

"If you're wondering how long I've lived here," he responded, a sly grin reaching his firm cheekbones, "I'm a Cold native. Born and raised here."

"So, you were here when everything with the Cold-Hearted Killer went down?"

"When the first girl went missing, I was still living at home while taking Criminal Justice courses at Montana Tech. But I wasn't here when…" He trailed off for a moment, and I had a feeling his silent thoughts revolved around Grace's death. "I had just started the Police Academy when everything went down," he added.

"Were you close with anyone involved?"

He nodded, but his voice was otherwise silent.

"I'm so sorry, Dane."

"Me too."

The car grew quiet, and I gave him his space. Obviously, I wanted as much information as he was willing to give, but I wasn't going to be a pushy, insensitive bitch about it. I understood the tragic events that had led to Grace's death had left quite the scar on the entire Cold community.

"I knew nearly everyone involved," he stated, breaking the silence with his quiet yet firm voice. "The victims, two of the girls, I went to high school with, and I knew Grace Murphy. Hell, I even knew Dr. Gaskins. He'd been my family's physician since I was a little boy."

"I still can't believe a man everyone trusted, essentially the entire town's doctor, ended up being the Cold-Hearted Killer."

A humorless laugh left his lips. "Don't forget, he was also our coroner at the time."

Immediately, my mind flashed back to the script.

INT: Cold Police Station, two days after the bodies of Carly Best and Victoria Carson are discovered. Grace walks into Chief Pulse's office.

GRACE
Have we received the autopsy reports yet, Chief?

CHIEF PULSE
Dr. Gaskins said to be patient. It might take seventy-two hours before we hear anything.

GRACE
Patient? **He wants me to be fucking patient? Two of our girls are dead. I won't be patient until I figure out who did this.**

Nausea clenched my gut. Not only had the serial killer been a trusted member of the community, he'd been the one examining the bodies of his own fucking victims.

"That's probably one of the most disturbing details of the case." Supposedly at peace, when in reality, they were actually still vulnerable.

"Yeah." Dane nodded in agreement. "The most twisted irony of all, the entire city voted him into that position, *practically unanimously*, about a year before he went on a goddamn killing spree."

"That is so fucked up."

"I guess that's why Hollywood decided they needed to make a movie about it, huh?"

"Yeah, I guess you're right." I shrugged nonchalantly, but on the inside, I felt like vomiting.

I felt nauseous for the women he'd murdered and then violated again while doing a goddamn autopsy on their bodies. I felt sad for the victims' families who'd lost their loved ones too soon. I felt sad for Grace and her family. I felt sad for the entire community of Cold. Even though it'd happened nearly six years ago, that tragedy had left a permanent wound. Their trust had been compromised.

And, like a train cycling back into the station, I once again felt sad for Levi.

I mean, I hated that getting him to talk to me about Grace felt harder than attempting a root canal on a drunk monkey, but at the same time, the more information I learned about the case, the more I understood this was fragile territory for everyone involved.

"Levi and Grace had known each other since they were kids," Dane said as he took a right at a stoplight that switched to green. "There were thick as thieves. And if I'd been Levi, I would've been tempted to quit the force and retire my badge. Lord knows he has enough money to live off of for the rest of his life."

I quirked my brow, and Dane glanced out of his periphery to find my confused expression.

"You don't know anything about Levi or his family?"

"Um, no." I shook my head. "It's safe to say our interactions are purely business-related. Anything we've discussed has mostly been about Grace and what happened with the Cold-Hearted Killer."

More lies. Soon, I feared my nose would start growing.

Levi still hadn't told me any-fucking-thing, but Dane didn't need to know that. Deep down, I hated lying to him, but I also needed him to keep talking.

"Levi's father owned half the damn town before he passed away two years ago," he said and pulled the cruiser to a stop at a red light. "Levi sold most of the land and the businesses back to the town for dirt-cheap prices, but it didn't matter. His inheritance is basically enough to buy Cold, Montana three times over and still have money left over. Hell, besides land, the only thing the Fox family still technically owns is Ruby Jane's, but…" He trailed off before adding an explanation.

My mind flicked back to the script.

INT: Walter Gaskins, sitting at the bar inside Ruby Jane's, drinking a beer, while people around him drink and chat. He notices two young lovers kissing at the back of the bar, and his fist clenches around his beer. The bartender, Lou, stops in front of him with a smile.

LOU
Thanks for fitting Celia in the other day, Doc.

WALTER
[nods]
Is she feeling better?

LOU
[flips a bar towel over his shoulder and smiles]
Yep. Tomorrow night, we'll be celebrating her being five years cancer-free.

WALTER
I'm glad for you guys, Lou. And I know, if Betty were still alive, she'd be celebrating with you.

LOU
[frowns over the memories of Walter's late wife, Betty]
Celia loved Betty like a sister. You know if you ever need anything, you just give us a call.

WALTER
Thanks, Lou. Means a lot.

LOU
[leans closer]
So, any news on the autopsy reports on Carly and Victoria?

WALTER
[laughs softly]
C'mon, Lou. You know I can't give you any of that information until Chief Pulse releases it to the public.

"Anyway," Dane said, pulling me from my thoughts. "It's safe to say Levi isn't a cop for the money."

I glanced at him and nodded, but my mind started spinning again with new questions.

For one, why was Levi still a cop?

I mean, he never seemed happy, that was for fucking sure. And according to Dane, Levi had more money than he knew what to do with.

Not only did his many moods give me whiplash, even the small tidbits about his life did.

I wanted to ask Dane more questions about Levi. For starters, was he a dick to everyone, or was it just me? Yeah, that question was definitely at the top of my list.

But the police radio crackled to life. "Officer Marx, are you ready to roll yet?"

Dane responded. "I'm ready, Dispatch."

"We have a possible burglary call from an eighty-five-year-old female located at 77 Lily Drive. 7-7 Lily Drive."

"10-4, Dispatch. I'm en route. ETA three minutes." Dane flipped on his lights and sirens and did a U-turn in the road, switching directions and heading southbound on one of the main roads within Cold.

"Hold on tight, Ivy," he said. "It might get a little bumpy."

I nodded and reached for the "oh shit" handle to steady myself.

Dane weaved us in and out of traffic, and once our tires hit snow-covered back roads, he flipped off his lights and sirens. Another minute or two, and he took a left onto a dirt road with a hand-painted sign that read Lily Drive.

Once he pulled the car to a stop in front of a small white house with beige shutters, he switched the engine off and hopped out of the driver's seat. Before shutting the door, he added, "Stay put, Ivy."

This time, I stayed inside and watched from the passenger seat as Dane walked in the direction of the house. He reached his fingers toward his belt, unclipped the stop snap of his holster, and left his right hand resting at the top of his gun.

Before Dane reached the front door of the house, another cruiser pulled up.

When Levi hopped out of the driver's seat, the word *fuck* fell from my lips on a mutter. I had the insane urge to slide beneath the dashboard so he couldn't see me, but it was too late. Our eyes locked as he walked in front of Dane's cruiser, and a scowl turned his lips down at the corners.

Oh, shit. He does not *look happy.*

CHAPTER TWELVE

Levi

FUCKING IVY STONE.

Everywhere I looked, everywhere I went, it felt like she was there. And now, she'd somehow managed to convince Dane to tote her Hollywood ass around Cold today.

The impulse to drag her out of his cruiser and toss her into mine *that fucking instant* was damn near overpowering, but I fought the urge and focused on the task at hand: a possible burglary call at Poppy Munn's house. I could drag Ivy's entitled ass all the way home when I was done.

Knowing Poppy's history of making frequent 9-1-1 calls over anything and everything, I wasn't on high alert. But a good police officer never assumed anything.

I walked toward the front porch where Dane stood talking to the eighty-five-year-old owner of the house.

"What's going on, Ms. Munn?" I asked as I closed the distance between us.

"It's okay, Levi," she called back, her arms gesturing wildly beneath her pink housecoat. Strands of her gray hair fell out of the messy knot on top of her head and into her eyes. She blew them away with an exaggerated breath.

I stepped onto the worn, wooden steps of the front porch, and Dane grinned at me over his shoulder.

"She heard some rustling outside and got scared." He nodded toward the two garbage cans sitting on the blacktop of her driveway. Both had been flipped to their sides, and trash remnants scattered the ground around them. "But it appears it was just a few coons digging through her trash."

Considering I'd yet to see an actual emergency occur at sweet old Poppy's house in the approximately one hundred trips I'd made out there, I wasn't surprised.

"I'm so sorry, boys," she apologized, and the crow's feet around her eyes crinkled. "I just got spooked again from those damn raccoons wanderin' around my house. Those little bastards think they have free rein over my trash cans." She twisted her mouth into a half frown, and immediately, Dane stepped in to reassure her.

"It's okay, Ms. Munn," he said, affection softening his voice.

She looked down at her feet and tapped her black velvet house shoes against the wooden porch stoop. "I guess I probably should've called animal control instead of 9-1-1, huh?"

Animal control in Cold, Montana consisted of a man named Butch with one lone pickup truck. His retirement from the job was ten years overdue, and he had about a fifteen percent follow-through rate on calls. The odds of his handling her raccoon situation were slim-to-none. She'd probably have a better shot at the coons finding another person's garbage to fixate on.

I offered a soft smile. "We'd rather you call us and it not be an emergency, than you not call us and something bad happen."

She nodded, but her gaze stayed fixated on her slippers.

"Our priority is to make sure you feel safe, Ms. Munn." I reached out my hand and gently patted her small shoulder. "Never forget that, okay?"

"Okay," she answered quietly. "Can I get you boys anything to eat or drink for your trouble?" she asked, and her hopeful gaze lifted from the ground and back to us. "I just put a pot of vegetable soup on the stove. Should be ready in about thirty minutes or so."

"You're a sweetheart, Ms. Munn, but I'm going to have to pass," I said, and she smiled, the remnants of her embarrassment still coloring her cheeks. "Now, go on inside and enjoy your lunch, but let Officer Marx take a quick look around just to be sure everything's all right."

Dane looked at me with confusion in his eyes, but he followed my order and walked inside Poppy's house. The screen door shut behind him with a creak and a clank, and I didn't think twice about my next destination.

Off the porch and down the driveway, I strode toward Dane's cruiser where Ivy sat in the passenger seat. Just seeing her sitting there, looking back at me as I moved toward her, was enough to damn near put me over the edge.

This woman had some fucking nerve.

Even though she was involved in some big Hollywood film, she was not entitled to *anything* related to my police department, including a ride along with a rookie cop. One she certainly had zero permission for.

With my hands clenched around the handle, I pulled open the door and glared down at her. "Get out of the car, Ivy," I spat.

"No," she snapped back, her voice equal parts confused and irritated.

"You can't just walk into a police department and think you can do whatever the fuck you want without getting permission," I stated firmly. "We both know you're not supposed to be with Marx. Not you or anyone on your fucking film production received any kind of approval for this. Get out of the car. *Now.*"

"And what exactly am I supposed to do, *Officer Fox*?" Her green eyes darkened three shades, and anger dripped from each word. "Walk home in ten-degree weather?"

God, this woman was a pain in my ass.

"Get out of the car, Ivy," I said for the third fucking time. "You're with me. I'm driving you home."

"Oh, that's real rich." A sarcastic laugh left her full, pink lips, and I hated myself for how much I enjoyed watching them move. "The only reason I'm with Officer Marx is because you won't let me do my job. Which, we both know, me *and my fucking film production* did receive approval for."

"What's going on?" Dane asked, taking both Ivy and me by surprise.

I had been so damn focused on her that I hadn't even noticed his arrival.

"Everything okay?" he reworded his question when silence consumed the space between the three of us.

"I don't know what she's told you, but she isn't supposed to be riding along with anyone besides me," I said. "And that's a direct order from the chief."

He looked between the two of us, misunderstanding furrowing the lines of his brow. "I thought—" He started to respond, but Ivy's voice stopped him before he could get started.

"Oh, for fuck's sake," she muttered and stood to her feet. "I'm sorry, Dane. You're a good guy, and this is my fault. I shouldn't have pulled you into the middle of this." She patted him on the shoulder. "Thank you for today. I really enjoyed it."

"It's okay." He smiled down at her. "And it was my pleasure, Ivy."

I clenched my fists at the familiarity between them, but before I could say or do anything else, she stalked away from us and toward my cruiser. The passenger door slammed shut behind her a moment later.

Dane's now concerned eyes met mine. "You all right?"

"Fine." *Even though this woman might be the death of me.*

"You sure?"

"Before I got here, Glen got a call over at the high school," I said by way of changing the subject. The last thing I needed was the rookie's scrutiny. "Apparently, a fistfight broke out between a few of the boys. Head over there and make sure he doesn't need any help."

"Roger that," he responded, and since I was technically his superior, he didn't question me further.

By the time I reached my driver's-side door, the rookie's wheels were already rolling toward Cold High.

Without even glancing in Ivy's direction, I got into my cruiser and started the engine. We were back on the road a moment later, and my ears started to buzz from the deafening, tension-filled silence that stretched between us.

It only took five minutes of driving for her to be the first one to break the ice.

"What is your fucking problem?" Her fiery words cut into my skin like a blade.

"*You*," I spat back. "You are my problem." I gripped the leather of the steering wheel tightly, flexing my fingers around it a few times before taking a right back onto the main road.

"That's hilarious *and* ironic," she said sarcastically, and I bristled.

"And why is that?"

"Because *you* are my fucking problem *too*."

"Wow. You've got a dirty fucking mouth, Ivy Stone. I would've thought a woman of Hollywood had more class than that."

She laughed. It wasn't the least bit amused, though. "That's rich coming from the man who just made a scene back there in an elderly woman's driveway."

"I didn't make a scene. I fixed a problem."

"The only problem is that you won't follow orders and refuse to give me any information about Grace Murphy."

"Because Grace Murphy isn't any of your business!"

"Yes, she is!" she exclaimed. "I'm well aware you don't like that this movie is being made. I understand that. But it is out of your control. All you can do now is help make sure we do Grace justice."

Do Grace justice. Fucking hell, this woman. She didn't know jack shit about the justice that Grace Murphy deserved. It didn't involve a Hollywood film, but it appeared I was the only one in this whole damn town who understood that.

I pulled my cruiser into the driveway of Grace's house, and the brakes squealed to a stop. I didn't say another word, just sat in silence, staring out toward the house and waiting for her to get out of my cruiser.

The less I said, the better.

But Ivy had other plans.

She slammed her fists down onto the dashboard. "Can't you realize you are making this more difficult than it needs to be?"

I glared at her, but she didn't stop.

"Avoiding me isn't solving anything!" she shouted. Her voice jumped around the inside of the car like a bouncy ball. "The film will still happen. This town is behind it. The chief is behind it. Even Grace's family is behind it."

God, I wanted her to *shut up*.

But she just kept going.

"You are making this impossible, Levi!"

One moment, her shouts had my eardrums ringing like a bell, and the next, I was reaching across the center console of my cruiser and pulling her toward me. Our mouths crashed together, and I fucking kissed her. *Hard.*

It wasn't premeditated. The kiss, the urge, the uncontrollable desire, it had come out of nowhere. One minute Ivy was on the other side of the cruiser, screaming at me with fury etching the normally soft lines of her lips, and the next, I was kissing her like a man starved for her perfect mouth with my hands clasped into the back of her silky red hair.

She didn't hesitate. *No.* She kissed me right back.

I was completely unprepared. You would think after the first time she'd kissed me and all of the hours I'd spent with her—watching her talk, laugh, smile, scowl—that I would've known all there was to know about her lips. But God, they were warm and soft, and for a brief moment in time, they obliterated every thought inside my head.

Her small hands found my shoulders, gripping so hard they pinched the skin through the fabric of my uniform, but I barely noticed. In the end, it meant she was pulling me closer—that was what mattered.

God, she tastes so good.

Hard and rough at first, but eventually, deep and slow, our tempo changed, but our rhythm was always in sync. Our tongues danced, lips moved, and her soft moans echoed inside the tight confines of the cruiser.

Desire and hunger roared inside my veins. I drew my tongue over her teeth and swallowed her groan of pleasure as we slid even closer to each other, no visible gap between us now.

I was on overdrive. Fully committed, totally invested, and a whole litany of things other than numb.

I didn't know how long we kissed.

All I knew was one moment, I'd felt like I was flying, my brain running wild with imagining what Ivy felt like beneath her clothes, and the next, I'd felt like I'd been doused with a bucket of ice water as she abruptly pulled away.

My heart pounded riotously inside of my chest as erratic breaths escaped my lungs in short pants.

"W-what was that for?" she asked on a breathless whisper, her eyes locked with mine.

I had no fucking idea. I could've made more sense out of an advanced calculus test than the reason for that kiss. I'd felt primal. Raw. Like I couldn't have stopped myself if I'd tried.

Her big, mesmerizing green eyes stared deep into mine, and the instant her front teeth nervously bit into the soft flesh of her bottom lip, I had to look away.

She was too much. *This*, whatever the fuck it was, was too much.

Out the driver's-side window I stared, swallowing hard against the sudden dryness in my throat.

"Levi?" Her voice was still a whisper. "What was that for?" she asked again.

Good and bad warred within me, but eventually, the bad won out and twisted and tainted my response. "To shut you up," I said, and even though the words didn't feel right leaving my mouth, I added, "Tit for tat, I guess."

I didn't even have to look at her, I *felt* her body stiffen up beside mine.

Seconds later and without any sort of response, Ivy was out of my cruiser and slamming the passenger door behind her. She stalked toward Grace's house, the heels of her shoes swift and slightly unsteady as she moved up the front porch.

When the front door fell closed, I hated that I felt the insane urge to follow her inside.

But I didn't.

CHAPTER THIRTEEN

Ivy

WHAT AN ASSHOLE*!* I MENTALLY SCREAMED AS I STRODE THROUGH the front door of my current home away from home and let the door slam shut behind me. Wood hit metal with a loud bang, and I cringed. It was one thing to be angry, but it was another to take that anger out on Grace's house.

"I'm sorry, Grace," I said quietly into the silent space of the living room. "I swear I'm not trying to tear down your adorable house. It's just that your friend Levi is a bit of a bastard…"

Even though I'd never had the opportunity to meet her, I had the odd sensation she would've laughed at that, and most likely, understood.

I wasn't sure if that was mere wishful thinking or the thoughts of a crazy person.

The engine of Levi's cruiser revved to life, and I heard his loud retreat from the driveway as he left the house like he'd just committed a crime and was hurrying away from the scene in a getaway car.

But kissing wasn't a crime.

If it was, then he wasn't the only guilty party in the equation.

I'd kissed him first. Then, he'd kissed me.

And both times, we'd gained no clarity, only more tension and confusion.

But good God, Levi had *kissed* me. It may have started out rash, impulsive, but once our lips had connected, it grew into something else. I had no idea what that something else was, but I knew we were both *involved*. The kiss took on an actual life as we both urged it further. The only reason I'd pulled away was because, as a rule, I forced myself to consider logic before taking off any clothing in any sexual encounter. I didn't have illusions that I needed to be in love or married to have sex, but using judgment was a hard boundary. But I'd been a millisecond away from stripping down to the literal bare necessities, and I didn't even like Levi. And I was pretty certain he didn't like me. That one moment of pussy-to-brain consultation had been enough to slam on the brakes.

But why did kissing him feel *so* fucking good?

I strode into the bedroom and slid off my boots, letting them fall to the hardwood floor with an unceremonious clatter.

I stared at myself in the mirror of the small vanity above the wooden dresser. Denial wasn't an option when the evidence was written all over my face.

Flushed skin.

Remnants of heat in my green eyes.

Swollen lips.

Pebbled nipples beneath my cream cashmere sweater.

Anger had left the building, and arousal had made its grand debut.

In my defense, it'd been a while since I'd had sex. My current dry spell had just reached the five-month mark. Sadly, the last time I'd had sex had been with my ex-boyfriend Marco who would forever go down as the reason why I stayed the fuck away from musicians, especially rock gods with wandering eyes.

And with work consuming my brain, it'd also been a while since I'd gotten myself off.

So, maybe this had nothing to do with Levi? Maybe I was just, like, generally horny?

Uh-huh…Keep telling yourself that…

I looked at myself in the mirror again and groaned in frustration. I was turned the fuck on, and it didn't take a genius to figure out what had inspired it.

More like who *had inspired it…*

God, this was a mindfuck. I mean, of all the men on the planet, my body decided to be attracted to the biggest dick of all.

With my body aching and throbbing and making its needs known, before I could stop myself, I removed my clothes, climbed onto the bed, and slid under the covers.

It started off hesitant. Slow. My brain still filled with confusion and uncertainty as I gently touched myself, running the tips of my fingers through my arousal.

My body loved the idea of an orgasm, but my mind was at war with the fact that Levi Fox was the inspiration behind it.

Just forget about him. Focus on the orgasm, Ivy. You need this. Using reason is great, but you're human and you have needs, *for shit's sake.*

I closed my eyes as my hand found the perfect rhythm.

Thoughts swirled inside my head, and every single one revolved around him.

And before I could stop myself, I was imagining what it could've been like had I not pulled away from that kiss. I fantasized about Levi's lips moving down my jaw, my neck, while his hands slid under my sweater.

Our kisses turn rough and erratic as we clumsily remove our clothes. My hands are shaking as I grab the hem of the sweater and pull it over my head, but the way he licks his lips steadies me.

I have no doubts he wants me and wants to fill his hands with the supple flesh of my breasts, but I want my hands on him more. I knock him out of the way and set to work, undoing the buckle of his belt, unclasping the button on his pants, and releasing all of the pressure on his bulge with a slide of the zipper.

I gasp as he unsheathes his hard cock from his pants and runs a hand from base to tip.

My body aches with anticipation, shaking nearly violently as I move toward him and straddle his hips with my thighs. He doesn't waste a second, and he doesn't go gentle, poising his cock at my entrance and thrusting inside. Heat pools in his eyes as he slides out and inside of me again, stretching me, filling me, making me feel so good.

His lips are at my breasts, suckling and sucking and flicking his tongue against my sensitive nipples.

Our urgency sets our rhythm. Pounding. Hard. Delicious. And my eyes roll back in my head every time he drives forward.

His cock is oh so deep inside of me, and God, it feels so good. And we are so close. Both of us, panting, shaking, hearts pounding, racing toward each other's pleasure.

I moaned into the quiet bedroom. Like a glass of water being filled, pleasure built inside of me. The few seconds before the glass became too full, a switch flipped and I turned primal. Raw. I wasn't focused on anything else except the rising, inexplicable wave coursing through my body.

The glass reached its limits and overflowed.

Stars danced behind my eyes as the aroused nerves of my body hit their peak. I was melting and exploding at the same time. I didn't have any control, and I wasn't worried or confused or angry in that moment.

I wasn't anything but enjoying the ride, the complete release.

With every ounce of stress exorcised out of me, I lay in the bed, muscles relaxed and jellylike, heart still pounding and lungs slowly catching their breath.

It had all felt so right.

Until, it didn't.

A true fucking buzzkill called realization had started to set in until it became a blaring trumpet inside my head. The only reason it'd felt so good was because I'd been lost in my fantasy.

About Levi Fox.

CHAPTER FOURTEEN

Levi

"Fox!" Chief called from his office. "Come in here for a minute!"

Dutifully, I grabbed the fresh cup of coffee I'd just poured for myself and walked past a few of my fellow officers as I headed his way.

"See you out there?" Glen asked as I strolled past him, and I lifted my coffee mug up in a friendly gesture.

"I'm making sure I'm fully caffeinated for the four feet of snow we'll be working against."

Glen chuckled and nodded. "Should be a busy day."

It was a little after eight in the morning, and everyone was gearing up for the beginning of a new shift. Usually, four of us ran the morning shift, but today, we were blessed with five. In my opinion, more cops were always a good thing.

It sure as hell made backup calls much easier.

Not to mention we'd received a shit-ton of snow last night. Even though Cold natives were used to snowy conditions, excess snowfall still equated to more calls to the station.

Cars sliding off the road, Ms. Munn needing help getting out of her garage—you get the picture.

When I stepped into the chief's office, he sat focused behind his desk, his gaze never faltering from the scattered papers before him. "You need to head over to town hall," he said without lifting his gray eyes to meet mine.

"Town hall?"

"Yeah," he responded gruffly. "Boyce Williams called, and they're starting production on the movie today. They've set up shop in our town hall building, and they need you there as a consultant."

The previously relaxed muscles of my shoulders grew tense and tight.

"I'm on duty today, Chief."

"Not anymore."

Was he fucking with me?

"What do you mean, *not anymore?*" I questioned. My smartass tone finally made him look up to meet my eyes with his own.

"Exactly what I said. You're not on duty today." Terse and to the point, his words should've provided a warning, but anger had already clouded my judgment.

I was fucking pissed.

"Wow," I muttered, and a humorless laugh left my lips. "So, we're not only letting Hollywood take over our fucking town, we're also letting it get in the way of police work?"

Chief bristled. "Are you questioning my decisions?"

"Honestly, yes." *Not only yours but every-fucking-person's around me.* Lately, I'd felt like I was the only one using any goddamn sense.

"Let's get this straight right now…" He stood up from his seat and pointed his index finger directly at me. "You might be like a son to me and the best damn cop in my department, but you're not in charge here. While I respect any concerns my officers might have, I refuse to let your fucking demons get in the way of something important. And this film—it's important to everyone in this town. You might not be able to pull your head out of your ass to see that, but it is."

His words silenced me, but it didn't matter. He still had more to say.

"This story deserves to be told because it is important to this community and the memory of our girls."

Our girls. All five of them filled my head.

Carly Best. Only twenty-five at the time of her death. She had been quirky and sweet and could whip up the best blueberry pie in the state. She'd worked at her mother's bakery, and every time I'd gone in there to grab some pastries, her smile had brightened up the room.

Victoria Carson. Twenty-seven years old. Beautiful. Talented. Everyone in town had loved to go to Ruby Jane's just to hear her acoustic performances. Before she'd been murdered, our little community had been trying to get her to enter herself into the next American Idol *contest.*

Emily Morrow. Full of life, only twenty-five, and from what I'd learned, she'd been a strong pillar of the church community by teaching Bible study classes to the kids.

Bethany Johnson. She'd been like a sister to Grace…

I stopped myself before I headed down a familiar path that usually led to a bottle of Jack and oblivion. I wasn't a daily drinker, but sometimes, when the pain grew too strong, felt too real, I had to numb it before it choked me to death.

"I'm not the type of man to entertain outlandish bullshit just for the hell of it," Chief said. "If something ain't right, I'll stand my fucking ground and let it be known it ain't right." His eyes met mine. "And this movie *is* right, Levi."

Old Red was a man with character and a strong moral compass. He'd been an important male figure in my life. Hell, he'd been more of a father to me than my old man. Pulse had only ever done right by me.

He was generally a man of few words, but that was because he only ever gave the truth. He didn't put on airs, and he sure as shit wasn't easily impressed. And I couldn't deny that if he felt this movie was the right thing for our town, there was a good reason behind it.

That didn't mean I didn't fucking hate every minute of it; just that I couldn't avoid the inevitable.

Until this movie was done, Hollywood was here to stay.

"I'll let Glen know there's been a change for this morning's shift," he added, and without any sort of fanfare, Chief sat back down in his old leather chair and got back to working on whatever had had his focus when I'd first walked in.

I'd been dismissed.

And unless I wanted to really get on Old Red's bad side, I needed to suck it up and face the music.

I'd been hired as a consultant for that stupid fucking movie, and whether I liked it or not, that was the job I'd be doing today.

No police work. No keeping the peace and protecting my community.

Just a fucking Hollywood film based on one of the lowest points in my life.

One that still haunted me to this day.

If this wasn't the seventh circle of hell, I sure as shit didn't want to see the real thing.

max monroe

I hadn't wasted time changing out of my uniform, fearing if I made any sort of detour, I wouldn't follow through with actually coming. Of course, now that I was here, my mistake was obvious—surrounded by film crew, actors, actresses, and producers, I stood out like a polar bear on a tropical beach.

Cold's town hall was a beast of a building that usually appeared more abandoned than anything else. But now that production had set up shop in here, it was a totally different story.

It looked overfilled, bursting at the seams with movie sets, film equipment, and people in full motion—setting up cameras, adjusting lighting, and doing a whole bunch of other shit I knew zilch about.

It was surreal. Our usually quiet town hall might as well have been taken over by aliens.

What used to be an auditorium had been broken apart into a few sets, and one looked uncannily like the station. Every detail had been integrated and cloned, including the goddamn *Golden Girls* bobbleheads Mona kept on her desk.

It was eerie as fuck. And overwhelming.

Feeling out of place and unsure of where I was supposed to be, I slipped off my jacket and set it over an empty chair while I gained my bearings.

I hated that my eyes searched the room for a mane of red hair and bright green eyes.

And I outright despised the fact that I felt the inklings of disappointment when I didn't spot her anywhere in my vicinity.

But instead of focusing on the reasoning, I wrote it off as simple discomfort in unusual surrounds. I was just wanting to find at least one familiar face in the giant room.

Right.

"Levi Fox?" a man with a mess of gray hair and scrutinizing brown eyes asked as he stepped around three men setting up camera equipment and closed the distance between us.

I nodded and held back the sarcastic urge to glance down at the nameplate on my chest.

"Boyce Williams," he introduced himself, and we shook hands. "Producer and current man in charge until our director arrives in a few days."

Most people would probably say something along the lines of "Nice to meet you," but I felt no urge for pleasantries with this man—or anyone related to the production of this film, for that matter.

"Levi Fox. Apparently, I'm one of your consultants."

He smiled, nodded, and before another word left his lips, the walkie-talkie on his hip crackled to life.

"Boyce, we just got word that the props for the bedroom set won't be delivered for another two days."

Boyce sighed and held up one index finger in my direction. "Give me just a minute." He lifted the small walkie-talkie to his lips. "Hugo wants to start filming the bedroom scenes immediately when he arrives, and we need Johnny and Ivy to do a run-through before he gets here. Figure it the fuck out. Order new shit. Whatever you need to do to make sure it's ready by tomorrow."

He slid the walkie-talkie back into its holder, and his eyes met mine.

"Sorry about that," he said, but his words held no apology. It wasn't hard to deduce Boyce Williams was the type of man who didn't give many fucks about what anyone else thought or felt. And more importantly, he cared less about inconveniencing someone.

For lack of anything better to do, I just shrugged.

"I'd like to get you acquainted with Johnny Atkins today," he said. "He'll be playing, well, *you*, in the film." He grinned and gestured for me to follow his lead.

I knew who Johnny Atkins was. Hell, everyone in America knew the so-called "Hollywood Heartthrob." Women fawned over him like he was some sort of mythical Greek god, and men wanted to be him.

I, on the other hand, couldn't have cared less. The idea of meeting him sounded less appealing than getting all of my teeth pulled.

We walked past a few tables filled with food and refreshments, slowly stopping every so often so that Boyce could order a random fucker around, and eventually made it to the back corner of what used to be the town hall auditorium. Johnny Atkins stood in the center of a small group, smiling and chatting up a few women, who seemed to be more Hollywood Heartthrob groupies than anything else.

"Johnny." Boyce grabbed his attention, and Johnny turned his back to his fans.

I held back the urge to roll my eyes when a blond woman to his right sighed despondently at the loss of his attention.

The whole idea of fame was a real mindfuck for me. I never understood how people were placed on pedestals for shit like acting, music or sports. Why the fuck was any of it noteworthy?

"This is Levi Fox," Boyce introduced, and Johnny flashed his movie-star smile—all white teeth without the slightest imperfection. His blue eyes turned up at the corners as he grinned in my direction, but unnaturally, no wrinkles formed. He held out his hand to shake mine. I took it despite my discomfort.

"Nice to meet you, man."

"You too," I said, but the words felt like barbwire scraping across my tongue.

Nice was the exact opposite of what this felt like to me.

Annoying? Infuriating? A fucking thousand-pound weight on my shoulders? For sure.

But, nice? Not in the least.

"Levi is ours for the day," Boyce kindly interjected, and I felt like shoving that fucking walkie-talkie down his throat. "Feel free to pick his brain, ask him any questions you have about his character."

"Perfect." Johnny nodded in understanding. "Mind grabbing some coffee and chatting for a bit inside my trailer?"

"Not sure I have much choice," I responded, and both men laughed. Trust me, it wasn't in sympathy.

Johnny grinned. "Fantastic."

Yeah, real fucking fantastic, I thought as I followed his lead. This was the stuff dreams were made of.

I'd been inside Johnny Atkins's trailer for what felt like an eternity. In reality, it had only been about two hours, but the barrage of questions didn't make the slice of time go any quicker—or feel anymore enjoyable, for that matter. Question after question shot from his mouth at a rapid-fire pace, all of it related to me, Grace, and the Cold-Hearted Killer.

None of it was shit I wanted to rehash, but for the sake of being amicable and following the chief's pointed instructions, I gave my best impression of someone who didn't mind being there.

Besides cop and man with a permanent chip on his shoulder, I guessed acting could be added to my resume. Who would've thought?

"So, did you know Walter Gaskins?" he asked what had to be the one hundredth question of the day.

"Unfortunately, yes," I answered honestly. "Everyone in Cold knew Gaskins. Hell, most of them knew him because they trusted his medical advice."

"Was he your doctor too?"

"No." I shook my head.

"What about Grace's?"

Anxiety crept up from my stomach and urged my throat to spasm, but I managed to respond with a simple, "Yeah."

"Damn," Johnny muttered. "That's fucked up."

I nodded. *Yeah, and you don't even know the half of it.*

"Did you guys suspect him?"

"I didn't, no." *But Grace did. Too bad no one, including myself, listened until it was too fucking late.* My heart stung from the thoughts, and the taste of regret was potent on my tongue.

It'd been over five years, and still, some days, it felt like it'd just happened yesterday.

Johnny leaned back on the small leather couch inside his trailer, resting the ankle of one leg on the opposite knee. He looked at me as the wheels of his brain spun with what I could only assume were more fucking questions.

I silently hoped he'd switch the focus of his interrogation to something other than the Cold-Hearted Killer and Grace.

"So, you've lived in Cold your whole life?"

"Born and raised."

"Grace too?"

"Yeah. We had been friends since we were kids."

"And that's all you were together?"

I quirked a brow. "Huh?"

"Just friends?" He reworded his question. "Nothing more than that?"

Where in the fuck had that come from?

I squinted my eyes and stared directly into his far too friendly gaze. "We were coworkers too," I answered pointedly, watching his expression closely.

He didn't flinch or falter, seemingly appeased with my response.

"So, from what I've heard, the Fox name is synonymous with money in this town. Is that true?"

I shrugged, admitting, "My father had built a relatively big empire in this town before he died."

What I didn't describe was that Lazarus Fox had been the prime example of the power greed held over people. Money had been his sole purpose in life, to the point that he'd been nonexistent for most of mine. Hell, my dad hadn't really become a semiconstant in my life until my mother left.

But it had been too late.

I'd already considered Chief Pulse more of a father than my own, and luckily, through his astute guidance, he had helped direct my life path from a rebellious teenager always looking for trouble to pass the time to an actual man. Someone who stood up for the right things and made a promise to serve and protect his community.

If only I would've held that promise for Grace.

Three knocks to Johnny's trailer door startled me out of my thoughts.

"Conference room. Two minutes. We're starting the read-through," a voice that I knew was Boyce Williams called from the other side of the white metal barrier.

I internally sighed in relief over the idea of a reprieve from this madness while Johnny Atkins did whatever it was actors did.

"Okay," Johnny called back.

But my relief was momentary.

"And bring Levi along!"

Fan-fucking-tastic. Could this day get any better?

Probably not, I mused.

Johnny smirked and stood from his spot on the leather sofa. "I guess we've been summoned."

"It appears that way," I said. Sarcasm dripped from my voice, but the Hollywood Heartthrob didn't notice. He seemed to be impervious to it, most likely stemming from the fact that Johnny Atkins lived inside Johnny Atkins's world—a place where he was king and anything and everything revolved around him. He'd been nice enough during our conversation, but that was all because it served him to be.

His mannerisms were cocky, his movie-star smile shone with egocentricity, and most importantly, he spoke to those around him like they were beneath him. When he'd asked his assistant to grab us coffee, he'd said it in a way that made her feel like she was the lucky one in the scenario.

As I followed his lead out of the trailer and toward town hall, I noted that his strides were leisurely. He was confident in the fact that everyone waited on him, and he needn't feel pressured to rush.

I silently wondered if this was how Johnny Atkins handled everything in his life.

Alarmingly, he reminded me a lot of my father. Lazarus Fox didn't wait for anyone, but he had absolutely no qualms about making someone wait on him. My dad had been that way his whole life, and it wasn't just in business; it had bled into his everyday life as well. Even to his own wife and kid.

A vision of fiery red and mesmerizing green filtered past my eyes as we stepped into the second-floor conference room. Ivy sat in the center seat around the long table, surrounded by fellow actors, crew members, and Boyce Williams, but she was the only one I could focus on—her and the two empty seats directly across from her. I hoped one of them wasn't intended to be my own.

She was engrossed in the script in her hands, her rosebud lips pursed and moving faintly as she read the words on the pages.

I hated how much I loved the sight of those lips. I could imagine them in a thousand different scenarios, feel them in a million different ways, and not a single one of either would be given anything less than an R rating.

"Johnny, Levi," Boyce called toward us from his spot at the head of the table. Of course, he pointed toward the two empty seats at the center.

Internally, I groaned. This was all I needed, sitting directly across from the one woman I couldn't stand but seemed incapable of keeping my eyes—*or hands*—off of.

Instantly, Ivy's eyes lifted from her script and met mine. We stared at each other for a long moment, neither one of us giving anything away, until I broke the contact and engrossed myself with settling into the seat beside Johnny.

But the break in contact was only brief, and when I looked across the table, her eyes met mine again. A million emotions crossed through the green pools. Irritation. Confusion. And something else I couldn't quite figure out.

I silently wondered what she was seeing in mine.

Generally, since I'd grown up and gained control of the rebel inside me, I was the kind of man who could keep his emotions close to the vest. But ever since Ivy Stone had stepped into Cold, she'd managed to bring out things in me I hadn't even known were possible.

After Grace, all I wanted was to stay numb.

But Ivy seemed hell-bent on making me feel too fucking much.

About Grace. About myself. About her.

Despite the shit I'd given her about being selected for the role based solely on appearance, I knew that wasn't really the case. The red hair and green eyes were a match, but that was the end of the road. Grace's features had been hard and cut, in contrast to her girlie interior. And aside from being a cop, she was all pink and hearts and flowers.

Ivy's features were softer—perfect gentle lines and subtle slopes. Her body was petite like Grace's, but much more of an hourglass, and she seemed to be all woman rather than girl. The only thing they really had in common was the power to make me vulnerable.

"Well, hey there, Ivy," Johnny said beside me, his voice full of cocky confidence and oozing the familiar charm I'd overheard him unleash on the women who'd been standing around him when we'd first met.

"Hi, Johnny," she responded, a soft, friendly smile cresting her lips. "How are you?"

I silently wondered if they'd already been in a movie together, and I wanted to gut-punch myself when I had the urge to utilize Google when I got home later.

That was the last thing I needed to do.

I didn't want to know more about her, and the less time I let her consume my thoughts, the better off I'd be.

"Better now that I'm sitting across from you," he cajoled, and the inklings of irritation started to slip into my veins. When it reached my fingers, I clenched my fists under the table.

I wished I could've said the idea of Johnny schmoozing Ivy didn't bother me.

I wished I could've been oblivious to it all and not been looking across the table for her reaction to his words.

But wishes and reality were two different fucking things.

Ivy's friendly smile didn't falter, but she didn't say anything in response to that. Her eyes flicked to mine before she averted her focus to the head of the table where Boyce was clearing his throat to get everyone's attention.

"Everyone, this is the real-life Levi Fox," Boyce announced and pointed directly toward me. "He'll be spending a lot of time with us to make sure we're not fucking things up too badly," he teased with smirking lips. "I expect everyone to go out of their way to make him feel comfortable on set."

Several people at the table looked in my direction and offered accommodating nods and smiles. A few even quickly introduced themselves. It was too many names, too many faces to remember, but I did my best to act amenable.

"All right," Boyce announced. "Now that we have the pleasantries out of the way, let's start our first official read-through for *Cold*. Hugo will be in town in a few days, and we all need to be on the same page for when we start filming. And I need to get everyone up to speed on the script changes."

I stared down at the script sitting in front of me.

And it was the sight of that very script that really brought it all home.

Hollywood was really making a movie based on something that had happened in my life. No doubt, the worst experience of my life. One I still hadn't found closure from. And now, I sat in a room full of actors and crew members who would be recreating it as a *story*.

My fucking story.

"Everyone refer to page fifteen," Boyce said, and the sounds of rustling paper echoed inside the room. "This is the first scene at Ruby Jane's, and you'll see we've made several dialogue changes, not only for Grace's character, but for Levi's as well."

Grace.

God, just hearing her name cross Boyce's lips flooded my veins with anxiety.

I didn't like that this movie was based on her and she wasn't here to give any input. She wasn't here to voice what she really thought about Walter Gaskins or the girls he'd killed.

If anyone knew this story, it was Grace.

For months, she had lived and breathed it.

And at the end, she'd died because of it.

The only saving grace I had in this scenario was that Hollywood didn't know the full story. They weren't privy to some of the facts that only Chief Pulse and I knew.

And I'd take those fucking facts to the grave.

"After a lot of deliberation, June and Hugo have decided that highlighting a romance aspect between Levi and Grace will really resonate with our audience."

Romance aspect?

I lifted my head and looked around the room, taking in the expressions of the people around me, but everyone appeared unfazed by that revelation. Even Ivy.

Her eyes, though…they were on me, and they were remorseful.

My heart pounded wildly inside my chest to the point that my ears starting ringing with each loud thud. I told myself I'd misheard him.

That those two words filling my head had been a figment of my imagination.

But I could only lie to myself for a moment or two.

"Hugo really wants to capture a friends-to-lovers layer inside this movie, so it's very important that we start rehearsing the initial bedroom scenes between Grace and Levi early on. Johnny, Ivy, I really need you two to be on the same page starting tomorrow. I think it would be good if you both found the time to sit down with one another over the next few days and ensure that the chemistry we need on screen is there."

Bedroom scenes. Chemistry. Lovers.

Why in the fuck was a romantic relationship involved in this movie?

Friends-to-lovers. Me *and* Grace.

I opened the goddamn script, and despite my better judgment, I started scouring through the pages.

My gut clenched, and I stopped scrolling when three words filled my view.

INT: Grace Murphy's bedroom. Grace and Levi, lying in bed together, after their first intimate moment together.

GRACE
[**quiet, lost in her thoughts**]

LEVI
[**pulls her on top of him and urges her gaze to him**]
Grace?

GRACE
[**whispers**]
Yeah?

LEVI
I love you.

GRACE
[breath catches and tears prick her eyes]
I love you too.

LEVI
[kisses her for a long, slow moment then whispers against her lips]
I've loved you since we were kids.

GRACE
[smiles through her tears]
Me too, Levi. So much.

What. The. Fuck?

My brain exploded and my vision blurred to fiery red, and it wasn't Ivy's hair.

No, it was anger. Pure, unadulterated, white-hot rage.

Hollywood was putting a twist on Grace's and my story without any of our permission. They didn't know *shit* about their so-called twist.

God, I hope they don't know.

I steeled my nerves and smashed them with reason. There was no way Boyce Williams and his cronies knew the *real* story. They were just taking liberties. Doing what they wanted. Making those precious dollars and making a mockery of us in the process.

Fuck Hollywood.

Fuck this fucking movie.

Fuck everyone in this goddamn room.

No one cared about the way this ill-advised movie was affecting my *life*.

Chatter droned on around the room, but I couldn't hear what they were saying. A full-out war of emotions was raging inside me, and it required all of my attention.

I wanted to stay amenable—mostly because I didn't want to piss off Old Red. He was a man I respected, one I loved as if he was my own father.

But I couldn't fucking stand the idea of being walked all over. I was just sitting here, letting these entitled film industry assholes do whatever they fucking wanted without any consequences for their decisions.

This was my life, my past, *my truth* they were fucking with.

Not theirs.

CHAPTER FIFTEEN

Ivy

Table read-throughs were a necessity of acting, but I always found them fairly painstaking and...well, boring.

My love and passion for this career were rooted in losing myself in my character, and those moments didn't happen during a monotonous read-through. When the cameras were rolling and I was consumed in a scene, I felt alive and fulfilled. There, in the world of someone else, I got to touch on a life unlived. A path unchosen. A whole different version of myself.

During a read-through, I still felt largely like Ivy Stone. And, hey, I liked her. She was a cool chick. But I knew her pretty well, and over the years, the excitement had dulled.

And that probably explained why I discreetly checked the screen of my phone while Boyce started to discuss business with the entire cast and crew.

It was on silent, but it had still vibrated its notification inside my pocket.

Under the table and out of everyone's view, I glanced down to find a text message from Sam Murphy, warmly known to me as Grandpa Sam.

Grace's grandfather had taken a liking to me ever since he and

Grace's mother Mary had reached out to welcome me to town, and lately, he'd made it a point to send me random little tidbits about his granddaughter.

Sam: Gracie hated peanut butter. I mean, HATED it. But she had a sweet tooth that rivaled a kid in a candy shop. The girl loved her sweets.

Now, I wouldn't say the information he provided was groundbreaking in my quest for character motivation by any means, but I couldn't deny I adored every single message I received. So far, he'd told me about her favorite movies, music, and the time he'd caught her "necking" in a car with a boy named Paul when she'd been a teenager.

He so obviously loved his granddaughter, even as the years after her death ticked away, and it warmed my heart that he was so welcoming and willing to share his memories of her.

I quickly—*and quietly*—tapped my fingers across the keypad and sent him a response while Boyce launched into a long explanation of the new script changes I'd already been privy to since I'd arrived in town before most of the cast.

Me: :) Grace and I definitely share a commonality when it comes to having a sweet tooth. Give me chocolate and pastries, and I am a happy girl.

Sam: Have you stopped by Luna Rae's yet?

Me: Luna Rae's?

Sam: The best damn bakery in Cold. Her bear claws and cheese crowns are to die for. You'll be addicted after one bite.

He also gave me little recommendations of things to do and eat in Cold. After I'd damn near melted into a puddle of gooey satisfaction after trying out his "best tacos in town" rec at a little mom-and-pop Mexican restaurant across the street from this very building, I knew I'd gained quite the inside source with him.

Me: Looks like Luna Rae and I will be introduced to one another very, very soon.

Sam: You won't regret it, darlin'.

I smiled at his response and slid my phone back into my pocket before bringing my eyes back to the table. Thanks to my inside knowledge, it wasn't hard to catch up to the conversation.

"I guess it's a good thing I kept up my training schedule from the MMA movie I just finished filming," Johnny said, smirking in a way only a man who was one hundred percent in love with himself could.

I knew immediately he was referring to the new "bedroom" scenes that had been added to the script. All three of them included Johnny and me wearing more skin than clothes, and he was an egomaniac.

Of course Johnny was solely focused on how he'd look on camera instead of portraying our characters accurately. He gave zero fucks about the detour from the actual story our screenwriter and director had decided to take. He just wanted to make sure his abs were on point.

I fought the urge to roll my eyes. I'd never actually worked with Johnny, but a few of my closest actress friends had, and I'd heard plenty of stories to understand the kind of man he really was.

Boyce chuckled at his stupid comment. "Johnny, we're definitely going to be scheduling some sparring matches together over the next few months."

Johnny laughed. "Bring it, Boyce."

A fucking boys club of dick-comparing, these two.

Sometimes, being a woman of Hollywood was a lot harder than most realized. While Boyce would be praised for his six-pack abs and muscly biceps, I'd be scrutinized for any little fat roll that got captured on film.

Of course, I didn't want to look bloated and out of shape on camera, but I also wasn't going to reroute my focus toward my own personal vanity issues.

This story was about Grace Murphy.

And I knew in order to really portray the fierce, determined woman she had been, I needed to focus on her character. *Her life.* Not whether or not the cameras would catch the cellulite dimples on my ass.

"Well, I think adding the romance aspect to this story is fantastic," Johnny added and offered a mischievous smile in my direction.

I wanted to gag. I saw right through his persona. Sure, he was a fantastic actor, that I couldn't deny, but the man beneath the acting skills was purely vapid and narcissistic.

Levi cleared his throat, and my eyes immediately moved toward him. With tight tension lining his shoulders and a hard as stone jaw, every inch of his body bristled.

He looked pissed. And completely out of sorts.

"I have a quick question," he said through nearly gritted teeth. The normally tanned skin of his cheeks was glowing red with anger.

Ever since he'd stepped into the read-through with Johnny and sat down directly across from yours truly, I'd been trying so hard to avert my focus from him, even though every damn cell inside of my body wanted otherwise. And thanks to Grandpa Sam's short text message distraction, I'd been doing a pretty good job of it.

Well, until now.

Now, I couldn't look away. My eyes were solely fixated on him. My fingers trembled slightly as I lifted my glass of water to my lips to soothe my suddenly dry and scratchy throat. It was like his emotions had a live wire straight to my nerves.

I'd tried to pry an emotion other than rage loose from his vault on numerous occasions, thinking the anger was a wall carefully constructed to hide everything else—and I still did. But right now, the fury wasn't a front for something deeper—he was just pissed.

Boyce nodded toward him, smiling jovially, like a man without a care in the world. "I'm all ears, Levi."

Every single time I'd seen Levi's carefully controlled switch flip, I'd been on the receiving end of his ire. It was weird being on the outside looking in. My breath caught in my dry throat and held as Levi worked his teeth together roughly.

"What made you guys decide to add a romance element to this movie?" he asked, and as each syllable left his lips, the irritation behind his words grew stronger and more apparent.

Well, at least, it did to me. Everyone around us didn't appear all that tuned in to the bristling man in the Cold Police Department uniform.

What the hell is it that makes us feel so freakishly connected?

"Well," Boyce started to respond, seemingly oblivious that Levi looked two seconds away from going Hulk Smash and flipping over the table. "June Gatto and Hugo Roman felt like there was something missing for our female moviegoers. And after careful consideration, they decided that adding a romance element, even if it isn't a factual part of the story, was a necessary evil."

I hadn't thought it was possible, but Levi's jaw hardened more. Another fraction of an inch, and I feared it might actually turn to stone. "You didn't think women would be able to relate to the strength and determination that Grace Murphy showed in stopping Walter Gaskins? You didn't think that would be enough?"

"Of course we see that, Levi." Boyce smiled, but it didn't reach his eyes. "But we also know there needs to be a little more spice for the viewer's pleasure."

Levi sat frozen in his seat. His jaw was still hard, his lips firm, and his normally bright blue eyes as cold as ice.

I couldn't decide if he was at a loss for words or he was trying to restrain himself from throttling our producer. I poised at the edge of my seat, just in case I needed to do some sort of kicking herkie jump between them.

But Boyce didn't give Levi any time for a reaction. What he said was gospel, and now it was time to move on. I wasn't so sure the ticking time bomb of a cop at the center of the table would care about following the bullshit Hollywood protocol of voicing grievances quickly and then burying them deep, where they'd never see the light of day.

"All right," Boyce stated. "I'd like to do a quick run-through with set production to make sure we're ready to start rehearsing the first scenes tomorrow. Jerry, how are we doing on schedule?"

While Jerry, our head of set production started to ramble on with prop and lighting updates, I kept watch on Levi.

He was frozen in his seat, his eyes staring down at the opened script in front of him, and his hands flexed manically into fists and open again.

I wanted to ask him if he was all right, but I bit my tongue. I didn't want to make this situation worse than it already was.

But I didn't have much time to question my judgment.

Moments later, Levi wasn't frozen anymore. He stood up from his seat, the metal of the chair legs screeching across the tile. All eyes turned to him at the sound, and my throat closed around the unease. I wanted to fix this before he got himself into trouble.

His self-restraint proved worthy, however, as he kept the fireworks inside and mumbled "Excuse me" to the otherwise oblivious room.

And then, he was off, his strides long, fast, and hard as he stormed away from the table of still chattering people. He was out of the room between one heartbeat and the next.

I didn't even think after that. I just acted. On pure emotion, apparently.

I *had* to go to him. I had to make sure he was okay.

I didn't bother addressing the cast and crew; I just hopped out of my chair and jogged after him.

He was visible as I exited the room, his form cutting a dark and menacing line at the end of the hall. His fists clenched around a metal folding chair he'd found resting against the wall. Abruptly, he lifted it up, his movements a beautifully choreographed exercise in frustration, and tossed it from one side of the hall to the other. It hit the tile wainscoting with a shattering bang and clattered to the floor, bouncing wildly before settling. Any sane woman would have turned in the other direction—away from the big, bad man tossing furniture around—but I rarely controlled impulse with real sensible thought. Instead, I picked up my pace and sprinted directly toward him.

I didn't guard my movements as I reached him, grabbing the thick, muscled heat of his arm and squeezing. His blue eyes startled to mine in surprise.

"Follow me," I whispered. I could see the resistance swirling just under the surface of his pupils. They were dilated and intense, and I knew the real Levi wasn't even present. This man was pure emotion, and none of the problems between us existed. "Just follow me."

I needed to get him out of the hallway and somewhere private where he wasn't visible to prying eyes and nosy ears. Luckily, the hall had remained empty despite the ruckus, but I had a feeling if Levi kept throwing shit, it wouldn't be for long.

He stared down at me, my hand still gripping his bicep. My breathing shallowed as I prepared to go into battle, but somehow, some magical way, he didn't question or argue.

Without any words, I dragged him down the hall until we reached a darkened room at the end. I turned the rust-spotted knob of the closed door and, fortunately, it opened with ease.

stone

I ushered him inside quickly and shut and locked us safely away from the outside world.

The room was deserted. An *Office Space* version of an old Western ghost town, a worn, dusty desk rested in the corner of the room, flimsy cardboard boxes and old yellowed papers scattered across it.

Levi walked over to the desk while I watched. His shoulders were ridged, and the line of his back bowed. I bit my lip, mentally scrolling through the entirety of the English language, desperate to find some sort of word to comfort him. It was a painstaking process, and his wrath wouldn't wait. With both hands and a violent will, he shoved everything off of the desk with an angry growl. "Fuck!" he shouted, yellow papers fluttering and floating around him. "Fuck! Fuck! Fuck!"

Anger or not, his emotions stemmed from one thing: pain.

Grace Murphy had been important to him, and I couldn't imagine what it would be like to be in his shoes. She had been his friend, someone he'd known since he was a kid, and now, he had to watch as a Hollywood film picked apart their life story and made their own fucking version, no matter if it was factual or not.

He turned toward me, eyes still dark and haunted, jaw clenched. For as visually impactful as his desk clearing had been, it was unmistakably lacking in emotional satisfaction. "I can't fucking believe this." His voice was rough and open—so fucking cutting, I could feel the edge of his pain. Completely unbidden, tears stung at the base of my nose. "They're adding a *romance element* to Grace's and my story? What gives them the fucking right?"

"I don't know, Levi," I whispered and closed the distance between us. "I honestly don't know."

He watched me closely as I walked toward him, his back resting against the now empty desk. But he didn't try to stop me, and for maybe the first time ever, he didn't use me as a scapegoat. His body still and his gaze intent, he watched as my fingers moved to his arm again in a gesture of comfort.

"I feel like I'm living in the seventh circle of hell," he muttered more to himself than me, the physical contact between us the sole focus of his contemplation. "Like I'm in the middle of a nightmare I can't fucking wake up from."

Blood buzzed in my veins, and a whoosh blurred in my ears. For some reason, I had an inescapable need to ease his discomfort.

Everything else between us—the fights, the kissing, the nasty words we'd slung at one another—didn't matter in that moment.

I just wanted him to be okay.

"I'm so sorry, Levi," I whispered. My voice shook with sentiment, but the unsteadiness was worth it. Because his blue eyes lost their harsh glare as they lifted to mine. "I know I can't understand what you're feeling right now, but just know I agree with you on this. I tried to get them to change their mind."

"You agree with me on this?" The hardness of his jaw softened, and his lips went from pursed to parted. He stared at me, but it wasn't with scrutiny or judgment. It was with surprise—and a renewed consideration. Like, maybe, just maybe, I wasn't as bad as he'd thought.

"Of course I do," I whispered back. "This story isn't just some made-up screenplay for the sake of making money. This is a real story. A tragic story. It is yours and Grace's story. It is Cold, Montana's story. And I think it deserves to be told the way it really happened."

His eyes shuttered, closing off secrets with the pull of a curtain. I wondered at the timing and reason, but I had no time to linger.

"Then why are you still here?" he asked. "Why are you still going along with it?"

I knew it sounded crazy, but ever since I'd arrived in Cold, Montana, I felt like I needed to be here. Like some sort of magnet lay within the town's limits and pulled at my core. I thought carefully about my words, hoping to make him understand that.

stone

"Because no matter what I do, they will make this movie. I couldn't bear the thought of another actress taking this role and not understanding how important it is. I feel like I'm the only one who really cares about making sure Grace's story is told right."

"You thought about quitting?" he asked, his voice so quiet I wouldn't have heard it had we not been in the silent, vacant room.

I nodded.

"But you stayed?"

I nodded again. "Because of Grace." *And maybe because of you too.*

My thoughts urged my feet into action without a conscious decision, and with two careful steps, I moved even closer to him.

He did the same, each of us doing our part to close the short distance between us. By the time we stopped, our chests were mere inches away, and with blue looking into green, our gazes locked together in a vise.

Something shifted in him. I saw it in the way his eyes softened and the hard lines of his jaw calmed. The tension in his shoulders released, and my heart pounded wildly inside of my chest. My breath hitched as he moved both of his big, strong hands up my arms, shoulders, until they reached the tresses of my hair.

Silence stretched between us as we continued to stare at one another. We *couldn't* look away.

I didn't know who made the next move.

But one moment, we were looking at one another, and the next, our hands were pulling each other closer. Flesh on flesh, the final inch to connection was seamless. Our lips danced a familiar rhythm that I recognized as ours.

Hard. Rough. Our mouths melded together as if we were starved and each other's lips were a feast. His hands stayed in my hair, massaging his fingertips into my long locks while I dug my fingernails into the strong muscles of his shoulders.

I anchored myself in the grip of his hot, real flesh and let the rest go. The past, the reason we'd been thrown together, and all the excuses for why we wouldn't work.

It was here and now, and Levi felt like the air I needed to breathe.

Fuck, he tastes good.

And without understanding why, I wanted more.

This attraction, it felt otherworldly. Like it came from somewhere deep inside my soul and I couldn't deny it if I tried.

But right now, I wasn't denying it. And neither was he.

His hands moved down my arms again until they reached my hips, yanking at the small sliver of flesh left exposed at the bottom of my sweater. Pressure and contact turned to lifting, and my legs wrapped around his waist. He turned us around until my ass rested on the empty desk.

Goose bumps rose across my skin, and my nipples grew hard and sensitive beneath my bra as he kissed me deeper. I reciprocated, delving my tongue into his mouth and tasting the sweetness of his lips from the inside out.

I throbbed and ached, and I felt my panties grow damp with arousal.

Instinctually, my legs wrapped tighter around him in response, and my hips took on a mind of their own as they ground against him. I needed more. More contact, more teasing, more *pleasure*.

God, he was big. And hard. And I wanted to know what he looked like beneath his uniform pants. I wanted to know how he'd feel inside of me. My mouth, my pussy—I wanted to feel his heavy warmth everywhere.

I moaned and ground down harder against him when his lips moved down my cheek to my neck, to my collarbone.

He responded with a gruff, raspy groan.

My toes curled, and I felt instantly greedy to eat up all of his sexy sounds. Groans, moans, growls, screams—I craved each of them in vivid detail.

Three loud knocks rapped against the shut—*and thankfully, locked*—door before I could try to make my fantasies become reality.

We both startled, hands dropping away from each other like we were on fire. But our bodies were still connected, my legs still wrapped around his waist and his still-hard cock pressed against me.

"Hello?" someone asked from the other side of the door.

I pressed a finger to Levi's lips and shook my head in a "don't respond" gesture. The feel of his hot, wet flesh on my fingers made me shake.

The knob jostled, but whoever was on the other side was impatient. When there wasn't instant success, their footsteps echoed down the hallway, retreating away from the door.

"Shit," I slurred, still drugged with arousal. It was so potent, not fading at all with the time spent not kissing, that I forced myself to do an appraisal of why. His cock was still very much hard and pressed against the apex of my thighs. And even through my jeans, I could tell he was big and turned way the fuck on.

No wonder I feel so out of control. There'd been absolutely no pause for logic this time.

Shocked and confused, I disentangled myself from him, unwrapping my legs and letting them fall heavily open. He escaped immediately, and with two steps back, he put space between us and turned his back to me.

"Jesus Christ." He let out a deep breath and ran his hands roughly through his hair. It stood on end and shot out in several directions.

"What was that?" I asked on a whisper, desperate to end how alone I felt with only his back in view. His shoulders tensed—the weight of the world coming back in an instant.

"It was nothing."

Nothing. Like a knife straight to my heart, that word hurt more than any of the careless words Levi had ever said to me.

Nothing. What a line of bullshit. I knew I wasn't the only one on that desk damn near fucking with my clothes still on.

Now, it was my turn to bristle.

"Nothing?" I questioned and hopped off the desk. The sound of my boots hitting the floor was undeniable, but he didn't move. He still only had his back to offer, and the distant move only made rage seep into my veins.

"You know, you could be a fucking man and actually turn around and face me," I spat.

Calling a guy's manhood into question always got him moving, and Levi was no different.

He spun on his heels, his blue eyes finally finding mine. But there wasn't kindness twined in their depths, and there wasn't respect. His sneer was patronizing and filled with false bluster. One veined arm flexed as he grabbed crudely onto the bulge in his pants. "I'm pretty sure we both know I'm all fucking man, sweetheart."

My lip curled at the foul move. "Don't patronize me with nicknames, *sweetheart.*"

He laughed, but it was all wrong—cocky and disconnected, there was nothing left of the man I'd first brought into this room.

I didn't know what had happened. There was a reason we kept finding ourselves in situations like this. When it came to the laws of attraction, it was all pretty simple; you didn't just keep kissing someone you didn't want to be kissing.

"I know I wasn't the only one who felt something on that desk," I challenged. His face never changed. Emotionless and cutting, he was resolved to his new game.

"I didn't feel anything."

I glared, and one index finger went directly in front of his face. "You're so full of shit," I spat. "So fucking full of shit."

Quick as a bullet, he moved toward me, damn near lifting me off my feet and locking our lips in a kiss. *Again.*

Our mouths melded and moved, and when his tongue slipped past my lips to dance with mine, I moaned.

My brain swam with confusion and arousal and a million other things I couldn't figure out, but the one that was the most intense was *want*.

I wanted him to kiss me. I wanted him to keep kissing me.

But quicker than it started, he stopped it, and I was back on my feet, Levi staring down at me with that goddamn taunt of voided emotion.

"See? Nothing," he whispered. I felt his words clench my gut and slide up into my throat like a ball of sick.

I swallowed past the discomfort and fought for composure. He wouldn't break me. I wouldn't succumb to insecurity, and I wouldn't let go of what I knew was true. There were two people in this room, and goddammit, both of us were *involved*.

Cued by his obscene gesture, I made one of my own. His cock jumped in my hand as I reached out and squeezed it in the palm of my hand. His eyes flared and his jaw flexed. "You're a terrible actor, Levi Fox. I know I wasn't on that desk alone damn near fucking with my clothes on. You were there too, and no matter how much you want to deny it, you were feeling something."

He wrapped his fingers around my wrist and freed my grip with a yank. "Feeling like fucking and feeling something are two different things, *honey*."

"*Why* do I keep thinking you're something other than an asshole?" I seethed, ripping my wrist away. The flesh from under his hand was still white from the pressure.

I didn't dare confront what the vigor in his hold might mean.

Without looking back, I walked past him and out of the room.

Screw Levi Fox and his many goddamn moods.

I was *done* with his whiplash.

CHAPTER SIXTEEN

Levi

Ivy lay across the bed, her red hair fanned out across the white pillow beneath her head. Her green eyes sparkled and shone in the soft lighting, and she writhed beneath the sheets, her lips parted, her gaze growing hazy.

Soft moans filled my ears, and I grimaced.

I *hated* the view.

My reason for hating it had nothing to do with the visual of Ivy herself but the Hollywood Heartthrob strategically placing his hands all over Ivy's silky smooth skin.

Fuck, while I was making admissions of my loathing, I might as well cop to hating my *reason* for hating the view.

His hands were all over her, his fingers strategically sliding across the stunning planes of soft curves and flawless skin, and I was Roid Rage-level jealous. Out of my mind, clenching fists, overflowing with seething hate *jealous*.

Just two days ago, she'd had her hands on me and her tongue in my mouth, and I'd been a huge, spiteful dick.

God, she'd felt good. Her perfect ass in my hands. Her little hips grinding against me at a maddening pace. My hard cock nestled against her denim-covered pussy.

If we hadn't been interrupted, would I have stopped?

I doubted I wanted to know the real answer to that question.

"Grace," Johnny murmured into her ear, and I grimaced...*again.*

Under the layers of Johnny and Ivy and my rampant jealousy lay another connection I didn't want to face. Me and Grace.

I averted my eyes from the scene before me and ran a hand through my hair.

I just wanted to be numb. To my past. To my present. To my fucking future.

I didn't want to *feel* anything. I didn't want to rehash my mistakes with Grace and my responsibility for her fate, and I didn't like the nagging pull to try again. Relationships weren't for me. It'd been fucking proven.

Yeah, but that doesn't change the fact that you are feeling *something.*

With a mind of its own, my gaze moved back to the bed. I couldn't stop watching her.

I couldn't stop myself from imagining taking Johnny's place.

I couldn't stop myself from wondering what her *real* moans would sound like when I slid inside of her.

I wanted to know what she tasted like, how tight she'd feel around my cock. I wanted to know it *all.* Ivy fucking Stone had a very real effect on me.

God, I wish I could hate her for it.

"Cut!" Boyce called from his chair, pulling me from my incessant thoughts and giving my eyes a much-needed reprieve. He took off his headphones and walked over a few wire cables and onto the infamous set that was supposed to be Grace's bedroom.

It was a half-assed remake of her bedroom, by the way. Too dark. Too modern. It looked nothing like the light and airy, overly feminine bedroom it had been when she was alive. Where sleek white sheets currently lay, frilly pillowcases and a yellow-and-pink patched quilt would have been in their place.

And her nightstand wouldn't have been anywhere near that clean. If it were really her bedroom, that very same nightstand would've been cluttered with books, reading glasses, and the ridiculous retainer she used to wear because she was adorably obsessed with dental health and having the straightest teeth possible.

Honestly, I was thankful those little tidbits of Grace had remained private, information privy to only her nearest and dearest.

Well, at least, it had for now. Who knew if they'd end up adding that shit in later?

Seeing that I'd been on set as a liaison for the past few days while they started to run through scenes, I'd learned quickly that anything could change.

Even the storyline.

When it came to Grace's house, Ivy had an insider's view. And although the bedrooms had been redone by her mom, the living room and kitchen inside her old house were still one hundred percent Grace.

I'd yet to hear Ivy mention anything regarding the difference in décor from Grace's real home to the film set's portrayal. But it appeared she was sensitive to the details of Grace's life that should remain private. Either that, or she was oblivious.

I couldn't even question it; though, I knew it was the former.

Ivy had said she wanted to portray the strong, determined, and confident woman Grace had been. She wanted to *really* know her. Ever since she'd arrived in Cold, Montana, Ivy had done nothing but prove her honest motivations related to Grace's character time and time again.

Hell, she'd essentially stalked me at the station in hopes I'd talk to her about it all, about *her*.

And all I'd done was give her grief and misplaced anger.

I lifted a hand to my chest in a pathetic attempt to rub away the sudden discomfort growing beneath my rib cage.

"Listen, Ivy," Boyce droned, calling my attention. "We've gotta get through this scene if we're gonna be ready for Hugo to get here and start filming tomorrow."

A quick glance to the set found Boyce looking down at Ivy. She sat on the side of the queen-sized bed with a white sheet wrapped around her body like a cocoon. Her male costar stood confidently beside her, wearing nothing but a goddamn piece of nude-colored material over his cock.

Literally, the man was just standing there with barely an inch of fabric covering his body, and he smiled like he was doing everyone on set a favor by showing off that much skin on and *off* camera.

"I'm having a hard time understanding this scene," she responded. "It just feels out of place for what's going on in the actual story. It feels like it got tossed in here at random without any real thought behind it. I know we've switched gears to highlight a romance element to Grace and Levi, but the way this scene is laid out, it honestly feels off to me."

"Listen, honey." Boyce ran a hand through his pepper-gray hair. "I'm not sure if you're familiar with how movies are made, but we pay you to act out the script that we've provided, no more. Leave the writing to the writers and the producing—" He jerked a thumb at himself "—to the producers."

Wow. What an asshole. I stepped forward but stopped myself before

I did something stupid like walk onto the set and tell Boyce Williams to shove his condescending attitude up his ass.

He fucking deserved it, but it wasn't my place and I didn't want it to be.

Right?

Fuck, Levi. Focus.

My job was to stay amenable. Provide any information I could when asked, and otherwise, just sit back and watch Hollywood make a movie about my life, knowing I literally had no say in the matter.

"Please do not talk to me like that." Ivy stared steadily at him from her spot on the bed. "I'm not trying to be a pain in the ass. I'm trying to make sure this movie is what it should be. And I'm telling you, Boyce, no matter what you think, this scene is out of place. It's too fast for Grace and Levi. It feels rushed."

I found her analysis surprisingly insightful. And surprisingly accurate.

Fuck.

He pursed his lips, his annoyance visible on every inch of his puckered-up face.

He'd been in a mood since the day started, and I silently wondered if this would be his breaking point. He was a man who didn't like to be questioned. He gave the commands, and people followed. Period.

Ivy was throwing a big fucking wrench into that agenda.

"Let me worry about what this movie should or shouldn't be, and you just act out the fucking script you've been given," Boyce retorted. "And while we're taking a break from *getting work done*, the point of this scene is to show an intimate progression with Levi and Grace *and* to provide some sex appeal to our viewers. We can't do that when you've got yourself wrapped up in the goddamn sheets like a burrito. Less sheets, more skin, okay?"

Ivy's face morphed into disgust, but before she could respond, Boyce laid into her harder.

"I refuse to let an actress who is insecure—*because her ass is ten pounds bigger than it was during auditions*—to slow this production down," he stated snidely. "My job is to make sure we do *not* veer off our filming schedule. We have a lot of investors who will be severely displeased if we do."

Her strong, confident shoulders slowly sagged forward with each word that left his lips, and I wanted to throttle the insensitive piece of shit with my fist.

I'd never seen Ivy look anything but self-assured. Determined. Strong.

His words had broken her down into something far weaker and substantially more vulnerable. Pain shot through the space below my ribs and tightened my jaw.

Boyce, on the other hand, gave zero fucks. He felt no need to stop, and apparently, had no issues with laying into her in front of everyone on set.

And her costar, the self-centered asshole, didn't say a fucking word. He was too busy winking and smirking toward a few of the female crew members standing off to the side of the set.

"I know it's getting hard for you, seeing as you're twenty-eight and getting older by the day. And I understand it's hard to compete with the younger, *hotter,* female actresses of Hollywood, but we don't have time to deal with insecurity bullshit, honey," Boyce continued. "But I promise you, while we're filming, Hugo and I will make sure we position you in such a way that the added pounds you've managed to gain over the past few months won't be so visible on the camera."

She didn't respond. The will to fight had left her, and her gaze stayed safely at her feet.

"Do we understand each other, Ivy?"

She just nodded, and I hated the fact that his ridiculous words had managed to break her down. Ivy had nothing to worry about when it came to her body.

Lush curves, svelte figure, she was a fucking goddess.

Ten measly pounds? What bullshit.

If anything, ten pounds would've only made her more luscious, more curvaceous, more perfect.

And she was young. *So* young. Inside or outside of Hollywood, her beauty was undeniable, no matter how much I didn't want it to be true.

She didn't deserve any of this.

I wanted to go to her. I wanted to save her like she'd saved me the other day, but Boyce stormed back to his chair behind the camera and plopped his ass down.

"Let's get back to it, everybody!" he shouted, and Ivy and Johnny didn't waste any time, slowly repositioning themselves on the bed in preparation for another run-through.

God, they were a stark contrast to one another. Johnny, confident in every aspect of the word, while Ivy's uncertainty, fragility, *discomfort* read like a neon flashing sign across her face.

She wasn't ready. But unfortunately for her, everyone else was.

"Action!" Boyce yelled, and the set grew quiet, only the sounds of the two actors on the bed filling the large space.

"I need to feel you," Johnny whispered toward her ear. "Let me feel you, Grace."

Ivy stared up at him, her mouth opening and closing, but no words came out. Her mind a million miles away and the lines she was supposed to say even further in the distance.

Johnny improvised, sliding his hands up her arms and into her hair, but Ivy's movements were stiff, her mouth brittle. She couldn't have looked any more disconnected if she tried.

When she clenched her eyes shut, Boyce's voice filled my ears on a harsh shout.

"Cut!"

Abruptly, he stood from his seat, and the clipboard that was resting in his lap fell to the concrete floor with a clanging thud. His long strides closed the distance to the set as he stormed toward the two actors adjusting themselves to a sitting position on the bed.

"Did you forget the line?" Boyce asked, his voice harsh with underlying accusations.

It was like he thought she was doing this on purpose.

Couldn't he see she was still reeling from his uncalled-for blowout a few minutes ago? Couldn't he see the vulnerability etched within the normally soft and sensual lines of her face?

She didn't look like the Ivy I had come to know.

She looked broken and battered, and fuck, it was awful.

I hated it. I hated every second of seeing her so fragile, so exposed, while all eyes were on her. Judging. Scrutinizing. Making comments under their breaths to one another while Boyce's anger stayed directed solely at Ivy.

"N-no," she muttered. "I—"

"You…what?" he questioned through gritted teeth. "What exactly is the problem here, Ivy?"

Enough.

Before I could stop myself, my feet were in motion, moving toward the set. And between one pounding heartbeat and the next, I was standing beside Ivy. She was still seated on the bed, only two scraps of nude-colored material covering her petite frame, leaving very little to the imagination.

God, she looked so small. So tiny. So unlike Ivy. My heart ached at the sight.

I lifted the sheet from the bed and wrapped it around her slender shoulders.

Boyce's glare turned toward me. "Can I help you with something?"

"Yeah," I said, locking my gaze with his. "I think it's pretty obvious to everyone here that she needs a minute."

"Excuse me?" he asked, outrage shining red and fiery from the depths of his gray eyes.

Thankful that his anger was now solely fixated on me, satisfaction spilled into my veins.

Yeah, fuck you, buddy. Your anger doesn't impress me. I feed on it. I breathe it. It's the only thing that gets me out of the bed in the morning these days.

"You heard me," I said. "She needs a minute."

Boyce stared back at me, slack-jawed. Anger vibrated from every inch of his body. "This isn't your place."

I ignored him and gently placed my hands on Ivy's arms as I helped ease her to a standing position. I fixed the sheet as she stood, ensuring that it covered her entire body. She deserved some fucking dignity in this moment.

Her eyes met mine, green gaze searching and uncertain at the same time. She was too lost inside her own head to rationally work through the situation.

But that was okay. She didn't have to. I would do it for her.

"This, *what you're doing right now*, isn't your place either," I responded, a calm quiet overtaking my voice. "I don't know much about filmmaking, but I'm sure your investors and director wouldn't be too keen on the fact that you're berating your lead actress until she can't physically finish a scene." I looked toward the rest of the crew on the set—the cameramen, the wardrobe team, the lighting crew—and all I saw staring back at me was understanding and relief.

The only person who appeared oblivious to it all was Johnny Atkins.

My eyes met Boyce's again. "And seeing that I'm the liaison between this town and the film, I can tell you that our board members and our community would not be okay with the way you're treating the actress who is portraying Grace Murphy. So, like I said before, she needs a minute," I repeated and led Ivy off the set without another word.

No one tried to stop us. Ivy stayed silent. And for once in her stubborn life, she just let me lead her without any questions.

When we reached her makeshift dressing room at the back of the first-floor hallway, she shuffled inside, the long white sheet dragging across the tile floor as she went.

The instant I shut the door behind us, her emotions boiled and simmered over until she couldn't hold them back any longer.

A myriad of feelings seeped from her pores. Anger. Sadness. Frustration. It was all there, in the firm, straight line of her lips, in the few tears dripping down her cheeks, and in the now-dimmed emerald of her normally bright eyes.

Silence overtook the space.

She paced the room, soft footsteps gliding on the new carpet, while I stayed standing near the door. It probably wasn't my place to be there, but I just couldn't find the strength to leave her like this.

The seconds bled into minutes, and eventually, once her tears had stopped and her foggy green eyes grew clear, she stopped in front of me.

"Why'd you do that?" she asked on a whisper, her gaze unrelenting as it searched mine for an answer.

"I couldn't not do it," I said. And that was the truth. We'd both been in that old office two days ago, and we both knew how it ended. I couldn't explain how we'd gotten from that moment to this one any more than she could.

She threw both hands out toward her sides. "What does that even mean?"

"I'm not sure."

She squinted her eyes, and I knew I had to give her more than what I'd been giving. I couldn't just slide everything under the rug and hope it'd go away. And more than that, she deserved to hear the truth from my lips, not some watered-down, numbed-out version of my own stubborn, angry, tortured making.

"I just didn't like seeing you look so vulnerable in front of all of those people," I said softly. "I couldn't not step in and protect you from that."

She didn't say a word, only stared up at me with those big green eyes of hers.

God, those eyes. They fucking slay me.

"You're beautiful, Ivy." For once, I gave her the truth. "So goddamn beautiful, and Boyce Williams is a fucking asshole for making you question it. Your face. Your body. Every fucking inch of you is conscientiously stunning."

"Oh, trust me, I know how you feel about *my appearance*," she retorted sarcastically. "You made it all pretty fucking clear when you let me know you would have no issues with fucking me. It's just that whole *feeling something* for me that's way out of your depth."

I grimaced. Fuck, I shouldn't have said that.

Not just because it made her feel bad, but because it was far from the actual truth.

It wasn't that I didn't feel something for her.

It was that I didn't *want* to feel something for her.

I'd lost all control of my feelings when I'd pulled over her speeding, stubborn, little white-lying ass when she'd first arrived in town.

I deserved her angered words and backlash. And more than that, she deserved my apology.

"I'm sorry about the other day," I said, and the forest green in her eyes softened to emerald. "I shouldn't have said that. You just…you *overwhelm* me." I let her see the remorse and discomfort I felt from those cruel words I'd said, exposing myself in a way I hadn't in years. "I'm sorry about a lot of things, Ivy. There's just so much more to this than you even realize."

I waited while she processed my words. It took more time than I was comfortable with, but thinking any amount of time would have felt differently was bullshit. It was the openness that simmered in me, not the time.

Eventually, she gave me a small, simple nod.

"Okay."

"Okay?" I asked, uncertain of her far too short response.

"Yeah, *okay*," she repeated. "I accept your apology."

A breath I didn't even know I was holding left my lungs. "Okay."

"Thank you for stepping in today." She wrapped the white sheet around herself tighter. "I really needed that."

Just like I needed you during the read-through…

I startled at my own thoughts.

Anxiety crept up my throat and clamped down on my voice box like a vise.

I felt like my brain was at war with itself. One side was wanting so badly to hate Ivy, not to feel anything related to her. But the other side was completely unable to follow through.

I looked down at her, and she looked up at me, her gaze open and vulnerable again, and oh so willing, but I couldn't reciprocate it. I couldn't give her anything else.

What I had already given felt like too much.

Two soft knocks to the door broke our eye contact.

"Ivy! You in there?" a female voice asked from the other side.

"Yeah."

"Boyce would like to know if you want to break for lunch or finish running through the scene first?"

"Uh…" She glanced at me and then back at the door. "Tell him I'll be out in two minutes."

Her eyes met mine again, but for as mesmerizing as they were, I found my gaze flitting briefly to her lips.

Fuck. She needed to get back on set, and I needed to put some distance between us before I did something crazy like kiss her again.

"I guess that's my cue," I said and turned toward the door, but her hand on my shoulder stopped me.

Our eyes met again, and my heart felt like it was pounding inside my throat.

"Thanks, Levi," she said. "Thank you for today."

"You're welcome," I responded, the words thick on my tongue.

She felt too close. I needed distance.

So, I found the much-needed space by leaving her dressing room.

But it didn't matter. The damage had already been done.

Ivy Stone was a permanent track in my life, and someone had set it to repeat.

CHAPTER SEVENTEEN

Ivy

I STRIPPED OUT OF MY CLOTHES AND STEPPED OVER THE EDGE OF THE TUB and under the hot spray of water from the shower head.

Ah yes. I nearly moaned.

There were two certainties in life: there was nothing better than a hot shower after working all day, and there were *no certainties* in this life.

There were possibilities. There were options. There were mistakes. There were a million "what-ifs?" But nothing was ever certain.

Over the past several weeks, I'd started to wrap my mind around Grace Murphy. I'd focused on understanding her, her motives, her personal convictions, her life, with the sole purpose of giving the most accurate portrayal of her that I could.

Now, with Hugo Roman, *Cold's* director, officially in the trenches of our production and two days into actual filming, I was starting to understand the whole "there were no certainties in life" sentiment. Despite the last-minute script changes and the blowouts with Boyce Williams and the everyday chaos that sometimes came with filming a movie, that realization had nothing to do with filming.

It was all Grace Murphy-motivated.

I was fully invested in her. I was living and breathing her. And the fact that one day she'd been on this earth, and the next she'd been gone was becoming a complex thing for my brain to comprehend.

She'd been a beautiful, special, amazing human being who was surrounded by a town of people who'd loved her dearly. She'd had aspirations. She'd had dreams.

At twenty-six years young, she'd had her whole life ahead of her.

But, in an instant, all of those things had been snuffed right out.

There are no certainties.

It was these kinds of realizations that could keep us up at night. They could consume us until we felt suffocated and helpless. Hell, I was pretty sure I'd freaked my sister Camilla out last night when we'd talked on the phone about the philosophical, life-related thoughts I'd been having while filming *Cold*.

"You're scaring me, Ivy," she'd said. *"Are you okay?"*

"I swear I'm fine," I'd responded. *"And these aren't bad realizations to have, Cami. They're soul-searching kinds of questions, and they're necessary to have from time to time. They make you realize that, although there are no certainties, we should savor every minute of this ride of life we're on."*

"Well…they sure as fuck feel depressing to me."

Her response had urged the corners of my lips to rise and a soft laugh from my throat. I'd quickly changed the subject after that, to my recent online Sephora splurge, as a matter-of-fact. Which, holy hell, it was a freaking mystery of the modern world how it was possible to spend so much on so little.

Makeup, man. That shit could make anyone go bankrupt.

By the way Camilla's tone had eased and a smile had made a reappearance in her voice, I'd known she'd appreciated the much cheerier change in conversation.

To her core, my sister was a real softie. She often avoided watching or reading the news just because it would take her days to shake stories of violence or tragedy. Where I was sometimes a little rougher around the edges, she was sensitive. I had a quick temper, and she hardly ever raised her voice. She was quiet as a mouse, and I could easily slide into boisterous and outspoken without any effort.

We might have been identical twins, but we were very, very different.

Opposite, but right.

In my opinion, a perfect mix. We rarely fought, and we balanced each other out. She could calm my red-hot-tempered ass down, and I had no qualms about doing whatever I needed to protect her fragile heart.

She might have been my assistant, but she was also my sister. My world.

It'd only taken me a good twenty minutes of being lost in my own head before I decided to actually *take* a shower versus just stand under the water. Quickly, and with efficient movements, I washed my hair, my body, and turned off the faucet before I used up all of the hot water.

I'd learned pretty quickly that Grace's house, while cozy and adorable, was old as fuck, and the water heater had probably seen better days.

Twenty plus minutes in the shower was pushing it.

Red splotches covered my freshly washed skin, and the delicious aroma of Herbal Essences shampoo permeated the bathroom. I'd been a fan of that product since I was a teenager and saw the commercials of the near-orgasmic women in the shower with their soapy hair piled high on their heads.

I guess I was a sucker for a good marketing campaign.

As I dried my body, slid off my towel, and slipped on my new favorite fleece robe I'd ordered off of Amazon, I realized there really *was* nothing better than a hot shower after working all day.

Twelve hours on set and even my bones ached with exhaustion.

stone

Hugo Roman, *Cold's* director, was a freaking workhorse.

I honestly had no idea when the man actually slept, and because of his workaholic tendencies, what should've been an eight-hour day had been extended an additional four hours.

We'd accomplished a lot, though. Despite the long hours, the day hadn't dragged. And I'd found myself so invested in the scenes we'd filmed, the time had passed at a rapid-fire pace.

Fatigue hadn't set in until I'd been in my rental and heading for home.

Prior to Hugo's arrival, things had been shaky with Boyce running the ship. The days had crawled by, and I'd felt like his oftentimes sour mood led to more chaos and blowups than anything else. It was no surprise, though. Boyce Williams was a certified dick to his core.

I cringed when a memory of him berating me on set—*in front of fucking everyone*—flashed before my eyes.

That'd been horrible. And so goddamn uncalled-for.

I had merely stated my concerns regarding the first intimate scene between Grace and Levi. But, obviously, Boyce hadn't taken the fact that I was voicing my opinion too well.

In fact, it had gone over as well as a fart in a beauty pageant.

With the heel of my foot resting on the edge of the tub, I squirted a healthy amount of my favorite lotion into my palms and rubbed it into my skin.

Thank God for Levi.

My eyes popped wide of their own accord, and I stopped my fingers mid-rub on the skin of my right thigh.

I honestly figured that was a first for me, giving thanks to Levi Fox for anything but being a pain in my ass. *Or a hot as fuck kisser.*

Good Lord. I shook my head at the ridiculousness of my mind's thoughts this evening and finished up with my lotion.

As I brushed my hair and stared at my reflection in the mirror, I couldn't deny that my annoyingly intuitive brain had a point. If it hadn't been for Levi stepping in the other day while Boyce had been losing his shit in front of everyone, I might've broken down right there in front of most of the cast and crew.

It would have been embarrassing.

But to my utter surprise, Levi had prevented that. He'd stood up for me. He'd understood that I'd needed to leave the set for a little bit and get myself in order.

Thank God for Levi.

Once Hugo had arrived, and I'd expressed my concerns about the first bedroom scene to him in private, away from eavesdropping ears and egotistical producers, he'd listened.

The end result? Rewrites. The first "bedroom scene" had changed from full-out sex to a deep, heady kiss that left both characters wanting more.

Kind of like that real-life first kiss with Levi…

And the second…

And the third…

Jesus. I wished my brain would just chill out on the Levi Fox thoughts.

Without any effort, I could picture his midnight blue eyes. The light scruff covering his jaw. The way his brow furrowed when he was irritated or focused. And the way his shoulders held so much power and so much pain at the same time. Most days, he looked like he was carrying a thousand pounds of tragedy.

And, if I closed my eyes, I could even picture his smile.

It was oh so rare, but God, it was a sight to behold.

Yeah, I need to get off this train of thought ASAP.

Hair brushed but still damp, I headed into the kitchen to make a "before bed" cup of coffee. Yeah, I knew it was a bit odd, drinking caffeine so late in the evening, but I was a world-class coffee addict. No amount of caffeine could keep me up at night. I could practically drink an espresso and still sleep like a baby.

Before I reached the coffeepot, my phone started vibrating across the counter, and I snatched it up before it vibrated itself right onto the floor.

Incoming Call: Grandpa Sam.

I smiled at the name and didn't think twice before hitting accept.

"Hi, Grandpa Sam," I greeted, all ears and smiles for his call. Over the past few weeks, I'd grown to love this man as if he were my own flesh and blood.

His gruff chuckle filled my ears. "Hello, Ms. Ivy."

"What are you doing up so late?" I asked, and he laughed softly again.

"Is this your way of calling me an old man?"

"Oh my God, *no*." It was my turn to laugh, and my cheeks heated with embarrassment at the same time. "It's just well after nine, and I thought…"

"And you thought an old man like me needs to be in bed before the ten o'clock news comes on?"

"You're so damn ornery, I swear," I retorted, and my cheeks puckered out from my tickled grin. "And that's not at all what I think or what I was trying to say. Give me a break, Grandpa Sam. I'm a bit exhausted from working all day."

"A-ha," he responded. "So, it looks like *you're* actually the old one in this scenario."

I giggled. "Yeah, technically, tonight, I am the old lady out of the two of us."

"First old, now a lady. What other things are you going to call me during this chat?"

"Oh my God," I said on an amused groan. "What can I help you with this fine evening, young, handsome, extremely manly and exuberantly never tired, Mr. Sam Murphy?"

He chuckled heartily. "Now, *that* is much, much better."

I swear to God, for an eighty-year-old man, he was a world-class flirt.

"I figured you'd enjoy that," I said and pulled the coffeepot out of the machine. As he continued to talk, I turned on the tap water and retrieved enough water for two cups.

"I actually have a reason for calling," he said, finally getting to the point. "I want to invite you somewhere tomorrow."

"Oh, really?" I asked, holding my cell to my ear with my shoulder and popping open a half-empty can of Folgers.

"It's somewhere special, and I would like for you to come," he said. "It would mean a lot to me, in fact."

How in the hell could I say no to that?

"Well," I started as I added a scoop of ground coffee into the filter and clicked the coffee machine on. "If it's important to you, then it is important to me."

"So, you'll go?" he asked, and I couldn't miss the hope in his voice.

"Just tell me the details, and I'll be there."

"It's tomorrow evening at Muldett's," he said.

"Muldett's?"

"The main banquet hall in Cold. About a mile up the road from town hall."

"Oh, okay." I nodded in understanding. Cold, Montana was basically the size of my pinkie toe, and it hadn't taken much for me to learn my way around town. "And what exactly is happening at this banquet hall?"

"It's a party. For Grace."

My brow lifted in surprise. *A party for Grace?*

"It's just a little tradition we've been doing since she passed," he added. "We have a party on her birthday to celebrate her life. It's been a good way for her mother and those who were closest to her—*me included*—to gain some closure in losing her so damn young. And Grace *loved* birthdays."

"Wow…" I paused and found myself at a loss for words.

It was overwhelming, honestly. I mean, for one, it was pretty amazing that Grace's family and friends did something like this to keep her memories alive, to keep her close to their hearts.

But I was just a stand-in for a movie. I wasn't sure how well I would fit into the equation that was her real-life family and friends.

"Don't overthink it, Ms. Ivy," he said softly into my ear. "I want you there. Grace's mom wants you there. Everyone wants you there. And like I said before, it would mean a lot to me if you'd come."

"Okay," I responded, but uncertainty clenched at my stomach.

Before I could express my concerns to him, three loud knocks on the front door damn near made me piss my pants.

"You still there, sweetheart?" he asked, and I nodded as I stared at the door.

What the hell? Who would be showing up here at nearly ten o'clock at night?

"Ivy?" Sam asked again, and seeing as we were on the phone, I quickly realized my nod wasn't a response he could hear.

"Shit," I muttered. "Sorry. I'm still here."

Three more knocks filled the otherwise quiet space of Grace's house.

"Hold on, someone is knocking at my door."

"Don't they know you're an old lady who goes to bed before ten?"

"Ha-ha, Sam. Funny," I retorted as I walked to the door with the phone still pressed to my ear. I figured it was best to keep him on the line while I figured out who was making a late-night stop.

Maybe it's Levi?

I ignored that thought and peeked out the window of the living room. It was pitch-black and I couldn't see a goddamn thing, but thankfully, a few moments later, another few knocks were followed by a very *familiar* voice yelling my name.

As I swung open the door, for some odd reason, my heart clenched slightly in disappointment.

But that quickly dissipated, replaced by the comforting vision of one of my favorite people in the whole world.

Same red hair. Matching emerald eyes. And a brilliant smile.

Camilla.

My assistant. My sister. A damn near reflection of me. My *twin*.

"Holy shit!" I exclaimed as she stood on the front porch with her rolling suitcase sitting beside her feet. "I thought you weren't coming for another few weeks?" My eyes narrowed. "What about all the shit you were doing for me in LA?"

She shrugged. "I figured you needed someone to keep you company out here in the middle of nowhere, and I forked most of it off on Mariah. I can't properly *assist* you from afar, now can I?"

"Oh my gosh!" I smiled as wide as Texas. "This is the best surprise ever!"

"Hello?" Sam's voice filled my ear, and I quickly remembered I was still holding my phone. "Everything okay, Ivy?"

"Oh, shit," I muttered and grabbed the handle of Camilla's suitcase and gestured for her to find solace from the frigid Montana weather inside the house. "Everything is fine," I said into the receiver as I shut the door and clicked the lock into place.

"Who's there?" he asked. "Sounds like you've got a special visitor."

"It's my sister, Camilla. She surprised me by coming into town a few weeks early."

"Aw, that's nice," he said with a smile in his voice. "Well, I'll let you go since you've got some catchin' up to do."

"Okay, Sam. I'll talk to you later."

"Oh, and bring that sister of yours along tomorrow night, okay?" he added, but it wasn't really a question. He offered a quick goodnight, and then the line clicked dead.

I set my phone down on the coffee table and wrapped my arms tightly around my sister with a giggle leaving my lips. "God, I'm so glad you're here. I missed you so much, Cami."

"I missed you too," she said and hugged me tighter. "I can't wait to hear about everything that's been going on the past several weeks. I feel so out of the loop!"

She released her hold and stepped back to look at me.

"Tell. Me. Everything. The people. The town. What in the hell you've been doing with your time? *Every-thing*," she added with a wink. "But first, I need to pee and get out of these jeans. Denim is never a good idea for a long trip."

I smiled knowingly and pointed toward the hall. "Bathroom is on the left. Your bedroom is at the end of the hall."

"Perfect."

"Oh!" she said as she took off her jacket and set it down on the edge of the couch. "Mom and Dad are a little pissed at you for only calling them *once* since you've been in Montana. You should probably give them a ring and let them know you're still alive and kicking."

"Whoops." I grimaced. "I guess I've been a bit busy."

Camilla just smirked. "Definitely call them tomorrow. I'm tired of hearing Mom bitch about it. Plus, they miss their second-favorite daughter."

I laughed, but melancholy flittered at the edges of my heart. I missed them too.

I was generally really good about keeping my folks in the loop, and usually, when I was away on location, I *wanted* to keep them in the loop. Phone calls with Dave and Helen Stone always made me feel better when things were stressful. Our little family of four was a tight-knit bunch, and it was very unlike me not to talk to them on at least a weekly basis.

But ever since I'd arrived in Cold, my usual tendencies had been derailed. My focus fixated somewhere else.

A sexy, brooding man with alpha-like tendencies and a badge.

As I watched Camilla grab her suitcase and get settled in, I couldn't ignore the pang inside my chest.

She wanted me to tell her everything, but ironically, the one thing I probably should've talked to her about, I didn't want to talk to her about.

Levi.

I had no idea what was happening between us. The other day, he'd rescued me. He'd been the white knight I hadn't even known I'd needed. And now, one thing was for certain—I couldn't get him off my mind.

But for some reason, I just couldn't talk to my sister about it yet.

I needed more time.

Time to understand it.

Time to figure it out.

Time to make sense of the strong feelings I'd so obviously developed for him, and time to see if he would turn on me again.

CHAPTER EIGHTEEN

Levi

I SHOULD'VE DRIVEN STRAIGHT HOME AFTER LEAVING THE STATION THIS evening. But instead, I found myself cruising around Cold in the dark of night. The glow of the moon, a few streetlamps, and the headlights of my truck were the only things left in the inky blackness.

I'd left work thirty minutes ago, and I was quickly starting to realize Cold was too damn small. If I kept making loops around the center of town, people would start to notice, and I needed to roam.

Yeah, I definitely should've just gone home. But lately, it seemed I was never doing any of the things I *should be* doing.

In the spirit of avoiding someone noticing my odd behavior, I took a right past town hall and found the open road.

Today had been a long day.

Before I'd gone into the station for an eight-hour shift, I'd worked on the set of *Cold* for a good five hours. I'd sat down with the director and discussed a few technical things related to police work, and then I'd had to sit beside him for what felt like an eternity as I watched Johnny and Ivy shoot sex scenes.

Watching her fake-fucking Johnny Atkins didn't sit well with me.

And *didn't sit well with me* was a really fucking nice way of saying torture.

I tried to tell myself it was because they were portraying Grace and me. I even tried to tell myself it was because I was merely annoyed with being on set and watching take after take of the same scene while hearing the same lines over and over again.

I failed.

Ivy was the one I was seeing in those scenes, not Grace, and I was mesmerized each and every goddamn time. She was alluring and beautiful, and her body was under someone else's.

It was a recipe for hostile psychological captivity.

So much so, even now, hours and hours later, I couldn't shake her out of my thoughts.

Another ten minutes into my drive and I pulled my truck to a stop just outside of the entrance to a driveway.

But it wasn't just any driveway.

When the logical, rational side of my brain caught up with the fact that I was outside of Grace's old house, which was now Ivy's current home away from home, I sighed heavily and rested my head against the back of my seat in defeat.

What the fuck, Levi?

From the street, I could see that most of the lights were still on inside.

She was home.

Quickly, I averted my gaze to the opposite side of the road while I berated myself. The last thing I needed to be doing was peeking in her windows like a fucking creep.

How in the hell had I ended up here?

And more than that, *why* was I here?

Because you want to see her.

The last time I'd really spoken to her had been inside of her dressing room right after I'd stepped onto set and told Boyce Williams, the spineless prick, to shut the fuck up.

Ivy had needed someone to stand up for her, and in that moment, I hadn't wanted that someone to be anyone else but me.

But once she'd calmed down and we'd talked behind closed doors, the way she'd made me feel had been far too much for my tortured soul to handle. I'd left without saying much more than a goodbye.

She pushed me out of my comfort zone, and I wasn't sure how to handle any of it.

Which was probably why my truck was currently sitting outside of her temporary residence.

With a heavy exhale escaping my lungs, I rested my forehead against the cold leather of the steering wheel as my truck idled in place.

Inside my head, my emotions, *these fucking feelings*, warred against one another.

Go to her.

You shouldn't be here.

But you obviously want *to be here.*

You can't *be here.*

It was too much. All of it. *Her.*

I had no idea what I was even wanting to get out of this. What good would it do if I just showed up in the middle of the night?

And what was the end goal? Talking?

stone

I nearly laughed at my irrational naïveté.

We wouldn't talk. We never *just* talked. Every interaction Ivy and I had, even when we were screaming at one another, was always so much more than us merely talking.

Before I gave myself any more time for impulsive, rash, *fucking insane behavior*, I wrapped my fingers around the shifter and slid it into drive.

Back the way I came, I drove ten miles over the speed limit down the mostly open road until I reached the center of town again and spotted the one and only place that had the power to provide some sort of solace.

As I pulled into the parking lot of Ruby Jane's, I turned off my truck and sighed quietly into the cab. Fatigue was starting to seep into my pores, and I needed a distraction in the form of a stiff drink.

The remnants of the several-hour discomfort I'd had to sit through while watching Ivy and Johnny fake-fuck each other on set, along with the overall exhaustion that was my constant emotional battle, sat inside my bones. And my appetite had been nonexistent all damn day.

Which was another reason why stopping at Ruby Jane's for a few hours was a good idea. I'd have a stiff drink, eat a burger and some fries, and call it a night once my mind stopped giving its best impression of a NASCAR driver.

My boots crunched across the gravel of the parking lot as I walked toward the front of the bar. Opening the big wooden door, I stepped inside. My senses were instantly kidnapped. There was noise and chatter and people. *Everywhere.*

The bar was far too busy for my liking, but I swallowed down my annoyance and nodded my greeting toward what felt like half the town as I headed straight for the bar.

Small talk and pleasantries were not on my agenda. My brain was far too muddled for that tonight.

The familiarity of the bar made thoughts of Grace swirl around my mind like wisps of smoke coming from a lit cigarette. The annual party the Murphys threw every year in honor of Grace's birthday was tomorrow—her *birthday* would have been tomorrow…

It was meant to remember her. To reminisce over the many memories we all shared with her. But every year, it only intensified the sting I still felt from her loss.

The jukebox in the back of the bar switched over to "Sweet Home Alabama," and several patrons shouted their approval. People cheered and danced and sang around me, and I couldn't fight off the scowl that furrowed my brow and pushed my lips into a firm line.

Normally, I could drown out the crowd. Ignore the constant chatter and boisterous voices. But as I sat down on the barstool and nodded toward Lou for my usual, my ears rang with aggravation. I felt hyperalert. Like every sound around me was being processed through a fucking megaphone.

Lou slid a whiskey toward me with a soft flick of his wrist. "Bottoms up."

"Cheers, man." I lifted my glass and nodded toward him before taking a hearty swig. The alcohol stung as it slid down my throat, and I shook off the afterburn as I set the glass back onto the bar.

"Everything all right?" Lou asked. "Haven't seen you around here in a while. Where ya been?"

I shrugged. "Well, considering I've been forced to take on another damn near full-time job in the name of a Hollywood film, it's safe to say I've been a little busy."

He scrutinized my face. I fought the impulse to cover it with my hands. I'd known Lou my whole life, and the man had a good sense of knowing when I was at war with myself.

Hell, on paper, he was my employee. Even though he physically ran

Ruby Jane's, I was the sole owner. It was the one and only thing I'd inherited from my father that I couldn't sell off.

Well, this, and that goddamn monstrosity of a house I currently called home.

"How's it goin' with that film?"

"Hell if I know. I'm just there to keep things *official,* courtesy of Old Red," I responded with another shrug, and Lou chuckled.

"Chief Pulse is a bit of a hard-ass, ain't he?"

I smiled. It felt like the first time in a year. "Preaching to the choir, Lou. I've been dealing with Red's *tendencies* my whole life."

He smiled and wiped off the counter with a damp rag before heading toward the opposite end of the bar to serve Butch Mason and his wife Amy Marie fresh beers.

I took another swig of my whiskey and stared up at the flat-screen television above the rows of liquor bottles that were ready and waiting to feed the alcohol lovers of Cold their favorite poison.

College basketball flashed across the screen, but I couldn't focus on anything going on in the game. I had no clue who was playing, who was winning, or how much time was left.

My mind might as well have been in China.

I only lasted another ten or so minutes before I decided that neither the whiskey nor the ambiance that was a boisterous Ruby Jane's crowd was going to quiet my racing thoughts.

Ideas of stiff drinks and burgers and fries were no longer appealing.

I just needed to go home. Take a shower. Go the fuck to bed.

I pulled a twenty-dollar bill from my wallet, tossed it onto the bar, and nodded a goodbye to Lou.

"You leaving already, Fox?" he called from the other end, and I offered a curt nod in his direction.

"Got an early day tomorrow," I explained as I got up from my barstool and pulled my jacket back on. "See ya around, Lou."

∎

Tired of thinking, tired of trying *not* to feel, tired of not being able to invite the numbness I'd relied on for the past several years, I made my way into the too big house that was my own.

I settled in, creating light and noise, but even with the rooms bright and the TV on, it was empty and far too quiet compared to the blaring thoughts of my mind.

I needed a distraction.

With my boots heavy and slow across the hardwood floor of my living room, I dragged my tired, out-of-sorts self into the hallway and straight into my master bedroom.

I was undressed and stepping past my half-filled walk-in closet and into the master bath scant minutes later.

The cream tile felt cool on my bare feet as I padded past the Jacuzzi tub and to the shower. I turned on the faucet and hopped inside before the water even had time to warm up.

It didn't matter, though. I couldn't feel a thing, not even the frigid temperature of the unheated water spraying across my aching skin.

I switched my brain to robotic mode, only focusing on the menial tasks of washing myself. *Grab soap. Wash skin. Grab shampoo. Wash hair.* I focused on the beautiful simplicity of each task.

And for a few easy moments, I found relief in that.

But it didn't take long for my thoughts to catch up to me.

stone

Visions of red hair and emerald orbs and a gaze so heated it could ignite my skin flickered and flashed behind my eyes.

My devious fucking hand found my cock after that.

And before I knew it, I was stroking my hand up and down my shaft as the sheer pleasure of it made my lids fall closed.

It felt good.

But she would feel better…

I stroked more, and my cock grew until I was rock hard in my palm.

Fuck, she's beautiful. Her rosebud mouth. Her striking green eyes. Her perfect fucking curves. The way her curvy little ass saunters from side to side as she walks.

My head swam, and I stroked harder, faster.

The sexiest woman I've ever known. Her body. Her face. The rasp of her seductive fucking voice. The way she moans when I slide my tongue into her mouth.

My legs shook as the pleasure of it all started to build. I rested my free hand against the stone of the shower wall to brace myself, while the other continued to move up and down my throbbing dick.

I want to feel her wrapped around my cock.

I want to hear her moans when I slide inside of her.

I kept fucking stroking myself. I couldn't stop. Didn't want to stop.

Yes, Ivy.

Fucking hell. I released my cock and slammed my fist against the wet stone wall as water dripped over my eyes and fogged my vision. I couldn't escape her. I couldn't stop thinking about her. She was consuming me, and I didn't understand why.

Because you feel something.

I shut my eyes, turned around and let my head fell back against the wall as the hot water sprayed directly into my face.

I had to stop this.

I refused to let myself get off to thoughts of Ivy. I feared, if I did, there would be no going back. Once I came to the mere idea of her, there would be no possibility of ignoring the feelings that were building inside of me.

She would consume me after that.

She already consumes you.

"Fuck!" I shouted, and my booming voice echoed off the walls of the bathroom.

I tried to distract myself. I tried to wash myself again in hopes I'd forget about her for more than a few fucking minutes.

But my cock was still hard.

And I couldn't stop picturing her mouth. Her mesmerizing eyes. Her fucking body.

With my hand to my dick again, a tingle running down the line of my spine and an ache in my balls, I was done. I fisted my cock, stroking once, twice, three times, and by the time I'd moved my hand up and down my cock for a measly thirty seconds, I came. *Hard.*

My knees shook. The waves of my pleasure rolled up my spine, and I shut my eyes as a deep, guttural groan left my throat.

It was wrong. But, God, it'd felt so good.

And the intense pleasure hadn't just come from the much-needed release.

No. It had come from the visuals. From the thoughts. The *fantasies.*

Of Ivy.

CHAPTER NINETEEN

Ivy

ALL EYES SWUNG TOWARD US LIKE A TETHER BALL THAT'D BEEN GIVEN a hearty smack as Camilla and I stepped inside the front door of the tiny banquet hall in town.

The walls were old wood panel and the floor a well-worn parquet. The combination of the two made everything blend together and added to the effect already set in motion by nearly fifty staring partygoers—the walls were closing in.

At least, in my mind they were.

In reality, the room was spacious and open, and nothing stood between us and the main space. As soon as you stepped through the front door, you were in the action.

"Okay," Camilla whispered, unwinding her scarf from around her neck and speaking only out of the very corner of her mouth. "Is it just me, or is everyone staring at us?"

The gawks of strangers weren't anything new in my celebrity life, but this was different. Wholly and fundamentally. The people in this room didn't find their fascination in my fashion or love life, but in the woman I'd been brought here to portray and my sister's and my resemblance to her.

Today's party was a celebration of Grace's life and its glory, both too short by a mile. She would have been thirty-two today, and I was a walking, breathing embodiment of everything she'd never be again.

An inch of my height disappeared as the sudden weight of skepticism and expectations settled on my shoulders.

I swallowed against the knot of extraneous saliva lodged in my throat and deflected. "Just surprised to see a celebrity, Cam. You should be used to this."

Cam, smart girl that she was, wasn't convinced by my pathetic attempt at brushing off the giant pink elephant in the room. Hell, we both might as well have been two *actual* elephants in a zoo, a crowd of people standing outside the clear plexiglass of our cage, watching our every move.

So I moved before she could dwell.

Quickly, I shucked my coat, gloves, and scarf, scooted to the front corner of the room, and hung them on a hanger next to the mishmash of outerwear already littering the front closet. Camilla's actions mirrored my own, delayed by only a few seconds.

But those few precious moments were useful as I stared at the simple movement of her arm and the flex of her muscle as she forced her coat between two others and took a deep breath.

Coming today had seemed like a good enough idea last night when Grace's grandfather had invited me—he'd been so convincing in his assertion that everyone wanted me there.

But the light of the banquet room was harsh and fluorescent, and all of the flaws I'd been blissfully unaware of during Grandpa Sam's pitch had developed a glare.

Some of the guests here weren't impressed by my appearance, wit, or credentials. In fact, some of them, I suspected, were only watching in wait—ready to see me fail. A few, I feared, were actually pained by my presence.

Internally, I was worried a lot of the people standing inside this banquet hall hated me. And if that was the case, their hate wasn't something I could control. It was solely because of my role in this film. I mean, my back-and-forth experience with Levi Fox wasn't exactly reassuring in that light.

Although, I doubted I'd be kissing or dry humping anyone here. I reserved that behavior for him.

"Just relax," Camilla coached like a little gnat in my ear. "Just be yourself, be kind, and be gracious. Everyone will settle into the weirdness, and then it won't feel strange anymore."

I nodded slightly.

I could do this. If only for the simple reason that I had to. I couldn't erase the fact that my presence probably came with a trip down memory lane for most of the people here, and I couldn't just walk out without saying a word. For better or worse, I had to weather this storm—for at least a little while.

Cam gave me a pat on the butt.

One slow step forward and then another, I forced myself to move toward the people, scanning the crowd for friendly faces as I did. I saw more smiles than scowls, and the reassurance helped some of the tension in my shoulders ebb. But for all of the friendliness, the search for familiarity was still alarmingly empty.

"I don't know who anyone is," I whispered. "I don't even see Sam anywhere."

Although I'd never actually met Grandpa Sam or Grace's mother, Mary, in person, I'd had the pleasure of seeing their faces about a week ago when Sam had decided to give FaceTiming a shot.

He'd been adorable, bumbling the screen around more than he'd kept it steady, and I was thankful for Mary's kind eyes and the way they'd instantly put me at ease.

"He's probably in the bathroom or something," Camilla advised. "Old guys have to pee a lot."

My face scrunched without instruction as I turned toward her. She shrugged. "What? He probably takes a water pill, Ivy. Those things make you run like a freaking hose."

I shook my head with a small smile, unable to keep it from making an appearance despite my disgust. "TMI, Cam. Wayyyy too much."

A throat cleared behind me, and I flushed, frozen. Heat tingled in my cheeks and numbed the tips of my fingers as my steady breathing flashed to erratic, and the abrupt loss of oxygen made it hard to retain full body function. There wasn't a doubt in my mind that whoever was polite enough to be alerting me to their presence from behind had heard the completely absurd conversation about diuretics. And now, I had no choice but to turn and face them.

My smile was brittle, forced at the edges and unnatural in shape, but it was there—I was an actress, after all. But Grace's mother's was radiant.

"Thank you so much for coming, Ivy. It's so nice to finally see you in person."

She reached for my hand, catching it in hers and squeezing it like a life preserver. I clasped back, fairly willing to let her take my hand and keep it if that would make her feel better.

Sure, I was Ivy Stone, a famous actress from Hollywood, but not to Mary. To Mary, I was the closest thing she'd seen to her daughter in years, and a kid to the nurturing yearn only a devastated mother could feel.

"It's so nice to see you too," I said and meant it with every ounce of my heart. "And I'm honored to be here. I completely understand that it can't be easy to—"

She shook her head, and the pinch of her hand grew tighter. I stopped speaking.

"No. I don't know that I can really even…" She paused, momentarily silenced by emotion. I fought against the sting in my nose and gave her all the strength my lowly hand had to offer. "You being here is good. Just…know that. I feel the closest I've felt to doing something for my daughter—something that *means* something for her—than I have since she died. People are going to know her again. Love her. Learn from her. She's finally got the chance to give them something I thought she'd never have."

My throat was thick as I answered. "I'm glad. I'm doing my best to do her justice."

Mary smiled wistfully, her mouth curling inward at the corners as she recalled a memory. "Grace was stubborn. Almost to the point of maddening. I'll catch myself sometimes, trying to glorify all of her best qualities and smear them over the flaws. But I'm always disappointed by how hollow it makes my daughter seem. She was real. She was flawed. And she was magnificent. Keep those things about her in mind, allow them in yourself, and I have no doubt you'll find a way to bring her to life."

Wow. That was *so* nice. Grace's mom was probably one of the coolest women I'd ever—

"What are we doing?" an elderly man's voice broke in from behind us. "Trying to resurrect a ghost?" I spun quickly to face the voice, but there was no actual satisfaction in it, and Grandpa Sam made sure to point it out. "Geez, girl. Slow down. Move that fast again, and you're liable to give *me* whiplash."

"Hi, Grandpa Sam," I said instead of arguing, smiling with genuine happiness at the opportunity to see him in person. We'd spent plenty of time calling and texting back and forth, but face-to-face contact, besides that one FaceTime call, had been nonexistent.

"Hey there, beauty." His eyes flashed to Camilla and back to me again, widening. "And there are two of you. Well, I'll be damned."

I laughed. "This is my twin sister, Camilla."

"It's nearly blinding, doll. The two of you standing together." Camilla and I both giggled at Sam's compliment. "We might have to separate the two of you. Just to prevent party casualties." I shook my head, and he spun me back around, throwing an arm around my shoulders. Mary was nowhere to be found, and instantly, I felt bad. God, I hoped she wasn't upset that I hadn't even—

"I can see your face headed straight for the ground like a plane on fire. Don't lose the smile now. I'm about to introduce you to some folks who need to be charmed to be won over."

Mary and my faux pas temporarily forgotten at his proclamation that I was about to meet people that didn't want to meet me, I froze. "What? Why would I go over there if they don't like me?"

He scoffed. "To win the fuckers over. Why else?"

"I really don't want to step on any toes here, Sam. I really appreciate you—"

"Hogwash. Sometimes you gotta stomp on some toes to really wake people up."

"Stomping on toes breaks them," I asserted.

He shrugged. "Eh, maybe. But it's necessary. If they don't break the toes, they don't go to the doctor. And if they don't go to the doctor, they don't mend."

My head spun trying to keep up. "What?"

"Forget it. Just be fucking charming, okay?"

"Holy moly, Sam. Dropping f-bombs now?" I questioned with a quirk to my brow, and he just smirked like the devil in response.

"F-bombs mean business in my book," he retorted, but his smirk was still intact. "Now, put on the charm and show these small-town folk what it's like to be in the presence of a celebrity."

Good Lord. I didn't like the sound of that. I didn't want the people in this community to see me as some entitled actress who thought she deserved the red carpet rolled out wherever she went. I wanted them to see *me*. I wanted them to understand I had taken on the role of Grace because it was important and I cared.

But I didn't have much choice in the matter because Sam was already in action.

I slapped a smile on my face, frail as it was. Jesus. Was I really about to go over there and talk to people who probably hated me?

Grandpa Sam's driving hand on my back was an undeniable answer.

Yes. Yes, I was.

God help me.

CHAPTER TWENTY

Levi

GIVEN THE CIRCUMSTANCES, I'D BEEN IN A RELATIVELY GOOD MOOD as I arrived at the farce of a birthday party Grace's family threw for her every year.

I'd always hated these things—the false happiness, the "celebration"—the reminder that Grace would never, in fact, turn a year older. It seemed like an exercise in masochism to me, to confront her mortality and the cruel end to it, with a party every year, but I'd promised myself I'd be more open-minded this time around. I'd take her family's obvious benefit from holding it to heart and try to understand the positives from their point of view.

My truck coughed as I switched off the engine with a turn of my wrist, and the whine of the hinges sang as I shoved open the door with a booted foot. I'd done my best to dress for the occasion in an outfit of jeans and a black flannel button-down shirt. It might not seem fancy, but Grace had told me she liked the way I looked in it on more than one occasion, and I thought honoring that would be in line with the event.

It made me remember her, it made her feel present, and it made me feel slightly protected from having an outburst by making her castigation seem vivid and current.

I could hear her coaching me to be calm, to smile more, to let go of the wrinkle between my eyes *before it stays there forever,* and *enjoy.*

Sure, she hadn't been easygoing in the end, when her obsession with the Cold-Hearted Killer and her best friend Bethany had taken over the entirety of her ambition and drive, but before that—before terror had found Cold—she'd been the light to my too often dark.

With slow and steady strides, I made my way to the door of Muldett's, the only banquet hall in town and the yearly location for Grace's party. It was an obvious choice, seeing as she'd insisted on having her parties here when she was alive too.

It wasn't exactly the Ritz, but it was the best attempt at fancy our town had to offer. And Grace had wanted fancy. The decorations, the food—she'd wanted it all to be something special. *A birthday isn't meant to be like every other day*, she'd always told me. *It's got to be special, cherished.* She'd always laugh then. *It's got to be something that keeps you interested in having more, even when you're pushing eighty and wrinkled like a prune.*

Hand on the cold door handle, I snapped back to the present and pushed it open. The room was big, but you could hardly tell for all the people overflowing it. There were familiar faces and ones I only saw once a year. People chatted in small groups while munching on food from paper plates, and kids ran through the legs of adults and played.

I'd only been inside for twenty seconds tops when Grace's mother's eyes caught my own and lit with a smile.

Mary Murphy was the epitome of poise. She handled hardship with the same graciousness as prosperity, and she was always the first to make me feel welcomed. I jerked my chin up in greeting and tried to thaw the hard set of my jaw along with the chill in my bones from the wind.

But it was still overwhelming.

This was still *hard*. Despite pep talks, despite good intention, despite time and effort—when I thought of Grace and all she could have been, I still *hurt*.

The coat on my shoulders felt suddenly claustrophobic, and the closet on the front left of the room called its respite.

I took it. Without thought or pause, I weaved through the crowd and pulled the sliding door open. Outerwear bloomed and mushroomed in the newly open space, and a quick survey revealed the lack of empty hangers. Not much for fashion or care of clothes, and more than ready to be rid of the stupid jacket, I balled it up and shoved it onto the shelf above.

If I could have found another way to stall, I'm sure I would have, but a tap on my shoulder signaled my alone time was officially over.

I turned slowly, my breath held in limbo between my mouth and my lungs, unable to escape or settle. It wasn't maintainable, I knew that, but maybe if I passed out, someone would drag me out of here and I wouldn't have to face it again until next year.

"Lee," Jeremy murmured as I turned, his voice easing the tension in my shoulders ever so slightly. Jeremy and his wife, Liza, I could handle.

"Hey, Jer." I took his hand in mine and shook it while giving him a stiff grab to the other shoulder. Liza shook her head at our very "bro" greeting and shuffled Jeremy out of the way to get to me.

With two delicate hands on my shoulders, she got up on her toes and put her soft lips to my cheek. I took her affection willingly, clinging to the closeness. I didn't allow many people to get close these days, especially women, and I certainly didn't invite them to stay in my personal space once they were there. I fucked occasionally, but I did it remotely, and I did it with strangers from another town. I didn't need sad eyes and knowing looks making me feel anything. When I fucked, the only feeling I wanted was in my dick.

Funny how the last time you fucked was before *Ivy Stone rolled into town,* my brain whispered, and I fought the urge to grimace at my traitorous thoughts.

Yeah, I'd been in a bit of a dry spell lately, but I didn't need nor did I feel like trying to understand why. Especially, now. It was definitely *not* the time or place to contemplate that kind of shit.

I didn't need to be an expert to know I was messed up, but fuck, getting close to someone sounded like signing their death certificate. It was all I knew, all I could remember, all I had to hold on to. I couldn't protect Grace, I couldn't go back and change anything, but I could sure as hell do my best to protect the rest of them.

Too bad Ivy is making that task feel impossible.

Silently, I chastised my own thoughts and wished my brain had an actual off button.

"I expected to see you this weekend," Liza said with a smile. "The girls have been asking for you ever since your babysitting beauty parlor."

I nodded at her and tried on a repentant smile. It wasn't one I utilized often, but for Liza and Jeremy, I could try. "I know. I'll try to come by soon. Work's been busy."

She eyed me warily, trying to read the level of my honesty and the red in my eyes. I knew she worried about me, but surprisingly, I hadn't been making all that many visits to the bottom of a bottle recently.

Jeremy wasn't nearly as concerned with being subtle. "I haven't been getting late-night phone calls lately. You haven't been driving, have you?"

Bristling at his insinuation seemed hormonal and basic, but I squashed it down. I owed this guy my life, several times over. I figured that also meant I owed him an explanation.

"Nah. Haven't been drinking too much." I decided to leave out the fact that one night I had. One night, I'd gotten out of my mind, and a little nothing of a woman with red hair and fierce green eyes had stepped up to take care of me.

Jeremy's smile was just as oblivious to those details as he was. "Good."

He grabbed my shoulder and squeezed but gave my eyes a reprieve. "That's real good."

"Yeah, well…" I said and then allowed myself a little laugh. Jeremy looked nearly startled at the sound. "Apparently, it turns me into even more of a bastard than I normally am."

Jeremy smirked. "Not true. You're a sweet drunk. Always telling me how much you love me and shit."

I shook my head with a grin and looked to my boots before giving him my eyes again. "For now, I'm gonna give not being any kind of a drunk a try."

Liza grabbed my hand and started to drag me away from the corner and the closet and safety. "I'm sure your liver thanks you. And so do I. Now I can concentrate on getting Jeremy to go down—"

"Do not finish that statement," Jeremy interrupted, and I nearly covered my ears.

"What?" Liza mocked innocently. "I was going to say go down*stairs* to get me chocolate cake in the middle of the night."

"Sure, you were."

Liza cocked an eyebrow at her husband saucily. "I didn't say *anything*. But if you're thinking something else, Jeremy Thompson, maybe you need to do something about that."

Jeremy turned to me for support, and I held up my hands. "Hey, don't look at me."

He huffed a little, annoyed that I'd ignored the bro-code, and turned to the room. I followed his gaze with my own, surveying the people with a small smile on my face.

And then it faded.

Jeremy and Liza, good friends from way back and privy to my many moods, sensed it and stayed silent.

In the center of the room, a crowd around her that only started to fray on the fourth row deep, Ivy Stone, Hollywood starlet, was holding court. Her smile was on full blast, and her fame glowed all around her. This wasn't the woman who'd started to infiltrate all of my carefully crafted layers—this was the woman who helped create them.

The vision of her, in all of her celebrity glory, felt like a punch straight to the gut.

Which persona of hers, I wondered, was the truth, and which was the lie?

"What the fuck?" I whispered harshly as she took out a pen and signed a napkin for Grace's uncle Phil.

Jeremy put a hand on my chest to stop my forward momentum. I looked down at it in surprise. I hadn't even realized I'd started moving.

"Relax, man. They're *excited* to see her. She was obviously invited."

"It's fucked," I snarled back. "This party isn't about *her*."

What was she doing? I mean, she had to know this party was meant to bring all of the people who had loved and known Grace closure. To bring them peace. To let them remember the far too young woman they'd loved so much.

Not turn into some goddamn autograph session to boost her ego.

Couldn't Ivy see what she was doing might as well have been a goddamn slap in the face to Grace's memory?

Sadness and confusion and anger flooded my veins. I felt like I was seeing some sort of mirage. Signing autographs? Taking selfies with fans? In the middle of a fucking remembrance party? She might as well have gone straight to the cemetery and spat on Grace Murphy's grave.

This version of Ivy Stone had me questioning everything I thought I knew about her.

"And it's not about you either," Jeremy reminded me. "If you want to express your dissatisfaction, do it later. Quietly. Don't make a scene."

I nodded, my thawed jaw hardening so quickly back to frozen. It'd felt good for the minute and a half I'd relaxed. Like I could breathe. Like letting the pain in my jaw ease had also eased the pain everywhere else.

Fucking lot of good it had done. Now, my anger felt doubled. I was mad for the showboating she was doing instead of honoring Grace, and I was mad at her for ruining my good mood. It seemed she was the root of my problems these days, and even though I might have forgotten that important fact for a little while, I'd do fucking well to remember it now. Especially, after seeing this.

Liza widened her eyes at Jeremy as I seethed, I could see it out of the corner of my own, but I didn't stick around to see more. Instead, I turned on a boot and headed in the other direction. Straight to the bar.

■

I was on my second glass of Jack when Jeremy joined me. He'd taken his time making an approach, giving me my space to get my head in order, but apparently, my pardon had been revoked.

"How about we have some water?" he asked. No segue, no gentleness. He was nearly as tired of my bullshit as I was.

I nodded. The movement was forced—stiff, even—but I knew it was the right thing. The last thing Grace's family needed was me coming in here and getting so drunk I dishonored them and their daughter. Not to mention, the fucking mess I'd make for myself.

Chief Pulse stared at me intently from the other side of the room, and I'd noticed Dane getting closer and closer as the minutes ticked by. Evidently, I needed a babysitter.

What a sad fucking showing.

I shoved the remainder of my glass of Jack at Jeremy, and he took it without delay. He knew not to squander an opportunity I'd offered. The more I drank, the less amenable I'd be to rational thought.

Ivy was still flitting, perhaps even oblivious to my presence. I could hear her voice as she floated around the room from one person to the next, but I denied myself the satisfaction of looking to see. I knew it would only fire me up again, and I was trying to calm down, for fuck's sake.

Why does she have to make me feel so much?

"Looks like Ivy is falling for Grandpa Sam," Jeremy remarked casually. And just like that—I looked.

Sam Murphy was a flirt if I'd ever met one, regardless of his age. He'd been that way since he was a teenager, at least, according to legend, and I suspected he'd be the same until the day he died.

Misplaced, misspent jealousy brought me to my feet.

Really, Levi? You're challenging the elderly now?

I sat back down. But I watched.

Ivy tossed her hair from side to side completely unconsciously as Sam made her laugh over and over again. The apples of her cheeks pinked with the exertion, and her toned arms crossed over her stomach in an effort to stop the ache.

Before I knew it, my feet were under me again, but this time…they moved.

One foot in front of the other and a swing in my arms, I matched the tempo of her laugh until it overwhelmed me.

I had a feeling the power of it would overwhelm anyone at this distance, though. Genius that I was, I'd stopped barely a foot away.

"Levi Fox!" Sam shouted, pulling me into a hug before I could spend any real time surveying Ivy's surprised face. I patted Grace's grandfather gingerly on the back and then stepped away to a safe distance—from everyone. "How are you, son?"

I nodded, letting the bob of my head fill in for the words I couldn't say. Verbally, all I managed was a grunted "Good."

"Do you know Miss Ivy?" he asked, smiling so big I thought his face might split in two. She'd obviously won him over beyond his normal flirting.

She answered for me when the words seemed lodged in my throat. "We've been working together. So, yes, Levi and I know each other well." Her voice was too kind, and I hated how easily it settled into my chest.

Unbidden, a flash of our bodies grinding together paralyzed my mind and numbed my lips. I knew the feel of her, the taste of her, and she knew the same about me. But beyond that, she didn't know shit.

I hadn't given her the opportunity.

Grandpa Sam smiled at the false news. "Oh, fantastic! Two of my favorite people, working together to remember—"

"We don't *really* know each other that well. Hard to get to know someone when you have next to nothing in common, I guess," I cut him off caustically before he could mention Grace. I tried not to, but the bite of the mix of memory and the present was too goddamn potent.

The hurt in Ivy's eyes at the sting of my words was even stronger.

"Uh, hi," a cheerful voice ventured from my side. I took a deep breath and turned to face the new arrival with a statement of dismissal, but everything in me did a double take.

It was Ivy's flesh and blood, vibrancy and beauty all over again. A hand moved over my heart subconsciously as I surveyed my sobriety. Had I had more to drink than I thought?

Ivy's double noticed the confusion on my face and offered a soft smile. "I get that look a lot." A soft laugh. "I'm Ivy's twin sister. Camilla."

She held out a hand for me to take, so innocuous in its intent, but two sets of eyes stared at it like it had teeth. The first set, I expected. They were my own.

But Ivy's, they were something else altogether.

She looked...*affected*.

Some evil part of me saw the opportunity to take advantage.

"Hi," I drawled, voice smooth and inviting. Her hand felt like sand in my own, rough and wrong and distinctly unfitting, but I steeled my nerves and settled on a course of action. With one half of an eye to Ivy, I smiled at her sister and treated her to a kindness I'd never shown Ivy personally. Hell, it was a kindness I'd probably never shown anyone, and I couldn't explain the reasoning.

I just knew that the way it made Ivy fall into herself made me feel good—vindicated. Even if it made the pain inside my chest grow at the same time. She was intent to worm her way into my life, my memories—my *details*. She thought it should be easier for me to watch her uncover the secrets of a woman who'd been a part of me. Maybe, if I did the same to her, if I forced myself into the cracks of her vulnerability, she'd know what it felt like.

I knew it was cruel, but that didn't mean I could stop myself from doing it.

"I'm Levi Fox," I introduced myself. "Ivy didn't tell me she was a twin."

Camilla smiled, her hand still in mine. I forced myself not to let it go. "She usually doesn't. But she is the popular one," she said, her words meant to tease her sister. "I'm just her lowly assistant."

I swallowed against the snide remarks begging to come out and focused. "Is that so? Well, I'll bet you're the nice sister. The good one." I winked. "The prettier one."

She blushed and looked to the ground, and like the dirty bastard I was, I took the opportunity to glance to Ivy. Her cheeks were ruddy and her eyes glassy, and Grandpa Sam had a supportive hand to her elbow. I wouldn't have noticed him had he not been attached to her with his touch, but confronted with his presence, I couldn't help but look to his eyes.

They were angry and knowing. He could sense the dangerous game I'd undertaken a mile away, and he didn't like it one bit.

The irony, of course, was that I wasn't enjoying it much either.

I just couldn't stop.

Noticing the plate of food in Camilla's hand for the first time, I softened my features and put a hand to the small of her back. "You want to go to the bar? Get a drink and have a place to put your food down?"

She nodded, the interest in her eyes growing with the addition of gratitude.

I put pressure to my hand as a guide and pushed her away from Sam and Ivy, and I did it without looking back.

I was already broken and bleeding. Visual confirmation of what I'd just done, what I'd sabotaged between Ivy and me, I feared, would be fatal.

CHAPTER TWENTY-ONE

Ivy

"So there I was, shoveling food down my throat, and he was introducing me to his best friend, Jeremy. Like I was something special," Camilla shouted from the bathroom while she washed her face.

My hands were shaking, and my eyes tingled with unshed tears from my spot under the afghan on the couch. I could see out the holes in the fabric, but it acted as a cloak for my emotions.

"Mm," I mumbled, barely loud enough to mean anything, but it was enough for Camilla. She was on a roll about Levi, and she didn't really need my participation. All she needed was a willing listener—and I was doing a good enough job of pretending to be that.

"Jeremy is so nice, by the way. So is his wife, Liza. Apparently, Levi babysits their kids—daughters—sometimes."

I smarted at the knowledge she had of him—knowledge I barely had; knowledge I'd only garnered by mistake.

My emotions were all over the place as I tried to lessen the violent turmoil inside.

Levi wasn't mine to claim. He was a jerk and a con and a fucking opportunist. He'd played on my weakness and the innocence of my sister today, and that made me want to cut off his air supply.

But Camilla was on a high from the royal tenderness with which he'd treated her, and the irrational part of me was jealous. Jealous of the unclouded joy she felt, as blameless as it was, and jealous of the man he'd been with her.

It was obvious by the way she spoke that it wasn't *all* an act. He'd given thought to her feelings and her comfort in a way that spoke to experience. He'd offered her a hand to get down from her stool at the bar, and he'd walked slowly with a mind to the length of her legs. He'd opened the door to the banquet hall to aid in her exit, and he'd held her hand to ease her journey over the slippery ice outside.

I'd fumbled my way behind them, Sam and Mary looking on with concerned eyes. I knew I'd looked sad, but I'd done my best to give them a smile anyway.

"He asked me all these insightful questions about my job and what it was like to be the woman behind the scenes," Camilla continued, completely unaware of my suffering.

Which was good.

None of this was her fault, and I had no interest in bursting her bubble. It didn't hurt anything for her to think Levi was good in all the ways that counted, and she didn't owe me anything. Levi and I weren't a couple, despite what all of the physical contact we'd managed had made it seem, and we weren't destined for one another. If anything, we were two peas in two very separate pods, better off without each other.

I just had to convince my heart to get on board the reality-bound train along with my brain.

Camilla exited the bathroom, flicking out the light behind her and plopping down on the couch next to me. I used the blanket as a shield—whether it was more active trying to keep her words out or my black mood in, I wasn't sure.

"So then he tells me about his mom and how she was this really proud, sure woman. Apparently, she left him and his dad when he was pretty young, intent to make something of her life. I don't know. I guess Cold was too small for her."

My head popped out of the blanket like a fucking groundhog at the shimmering, unheard news.

I knew next to nothing about Levi's family life after weeks of time together, but my sister had a whole fucking backstory after a single afternoon.

"Where'd she go?" I asked, unable to stop myself.

Her eyes got big and her voice, dramatic. "Get this. Hollywood. She wanted to be a star, he said."

I reeled, metaphorical arms whirling in an effort to stop myself from falling clear on my ass.

"Holy shit."

She nodded. "I know. There's so much irony. But he was pretty circumspect about it."

My eyebrows drew together, trying to picture Levi being cautious about anything. He certainly wasn't ever careful with my feelings.

"He went to the bathroom after that, but Jeremy's wife Liza filled me in a little. Evidently, Levi's dad was some big guy in town. Big money, big plans, that sort of thing. But he didn't give much attention to the wants of his wife. No one was really surprised when she left, trying to find other things."

"But she left her kid?" I snapped, disgust ripe in my voice. I couldn't stop myself from picturing a little version of the raven-haired, blue-eyed man I knew. He had to have felt so alone.

"I know," Camilla agreed, shrugging. "I guess some people mostly see themselves."

I nodded, but to say I was disengaged as a listener would be an understatement. I was too busy reshaping my view of the man I knew, all over again. Every time I stopped to breathe, it seemed like something else came out in his defense.

"Anyway…Levi came back, so we shut up about it then. We kept it light, and he asked me about how my time had been in Cold and if I missed home at all."

She sighed dreamily.

"He really cared what I had to say. I haven't had a conversation like that…you know, one that truly cared for my needs emotionally and physically…in a long time. God, probably forever, actually. Guys in LA are always such egocentric pricks."

I nodded again, swallowing back the vomit in my throat. Levi Fox had capabilities I never even expected. He had the power to be the kind of man a woman wanted forever. My body rebelled again, threating to hold my rational brain hostage in the emotional cage my little obsession with him had created.

But I fought. I wouldn't let the emotional nausea win. I refused.

I just had to face the facts.

Levi Fox, it seemed, was a gentleman.

He just had no interest in being one with me.

CHAPTER TWENTY-TWO

Levi

I'D SPENT THE FULL DAY AFTER GRACE'S POST-DEATH BIRTHDAY PARTY doing actual police work. As a police officer, as you might suspect, days doing such work were a regularity.

At least, they had been until recently.

Ever since Ivy and the film crew had come to town, I'd been spending way more days out of uniform than in it. Hell, I had three un-cashed checks from Trigate films sitting on my kitchen counter to prove it.

Thankfully, years of experience went a long way in making sure a little time off didn't make me rusty, and the good people of Cold had given me plenty of calls to keep me busy.

I'd been dispatched to Jeb Wilson's house after he and his brother got into yet another fight about milk cows.

Dairy cows, as a rule, have to be bred to maintain lactation, but the bull used isn't so cut-and-dried. Jeb and Jimmy had been fighting over which bull to use for decades. It's like a farmer's version of a football rivalry. And just like the bar on Monday nights, this set of adversaries often came to blows.

I'd pulled over a passerby in town named Tammy for doing fourteen over the speed limit in a school zone, and I'd been called to a possible robbery at the Pit Stop convenience store.

The robbery was actually a man in a hoodie with a pack of gum in his pocket, but I'd been dispatched all the same.

Several people in town had stopped to chat *at* me—and I did mean at.

It was amazing how little talking I could get away with in some of those conversations, but it seemed people were usually just looking for someone to listen. As a public servant, I made it a point to do so. Not when I had more pressing calls or public safety was in question, but when I was killing time between one call and another, absolutely.

After the pseudorobbery at the Pit Stop, a quick chat with town biddy and gossiper Hilda Vosser, and a short stint patrolling traffic, another call came in—on set.

Lights and sirens blaring, I hauled ass all the way there, worried about Ivy despite all my efforts to stop it. I didn't trust that fucking producer not to put his hands on her in anger.

I was half apoplectic by the time I got there, working myself into a cold sweat at the thought of Boyce's uninvited hands on Ivy in violence or *something else*, but in the end, it'd been nothing more than a false alarm, and Ivy wasn't even there.

They had a panic button-style system that sent an immediate notification to police, but it still had some kinks.

I told myself the call to the set was the moment I started thinking about Ivy.

The way I was hell-bent not to feel.

The way I'd treated her yesterday.

The dirty asshole I'd been by toying with her sister, just to get a rise out of her.

But the truth was, I'd been thinking about her all fucking day. For the first time in years, I felt the genuine urge to apologize.

It was one thing to hold her at a distance or to keep the private details of my life to myself, but it was another to actively, deceitfully antagonize her.

There was something to the passionate anger she made me feel, and admitting a need to confront it was the first step. I didn't suspect I'd be calling her to ask her on dates anytime soon, but I couldn't ignore her either.

Years of my life I'd spent as a walking zombie, but after a couple of weeks with Ivy Stone in town, comfortably numb was a memory.

I was angry. I was charged. I was passionate. I was *vibrant* again.

I was *living*.

And she was the reason.

When I came to the stop sign at the end of Tilly Lane—the last intersection between where I'd been and my house—I had a decision to make.

A right meant home. A left meant Ivy.

My tires didn't even stop rolling as I made my choice.

The road to home stretched before me like a beacon, and I put my foot to the throttle, eating pavement. This route was the rational choice, the safer one. This road was one I'd driven before and one I could predict. This was the way to the life I knew, the life I'd been living—to shelter, security, and nothing more.

I glanced in my rearview mirror for less than a second, but that was all it took.

That one moment of question. That one sliver of hope. That one reflection on what it would be like to have *more*.

My tires screeched, the pavement a sliding surface under the momentum of my cruiser. I barely had it stopped before I threw it into reverse and turned around.

The lights inside her house blared as I pulled up in the gravel drive outside, and my heart beat recklessly. It gave little thought to keeping rhythm and did a poor job of keeping itself from banging into the walls of my rib cage, but it was still pumping blood—and that was all I needed.

I pushed open my door and climbed to my feet, wildly trying to pin down a thought in my head. I didn't know what I planned to say, and I had quite a few doubts that if I managed to figure it out, she would want to hear it.

But I'd had this emotional epiphany without solicitation, and there was no going back. I couldn't force the feelings back inside, and I couldn't pretend she didn't affect me.

I climbed the porch steps and knocked three times, the wood of the door bouncing effortlessly off my knuckles.

"Coming!" she called from the other side, her footsteps audibly hurried. I took one deep breath and then another, coaching myself quickly as I did.

Be nice.

Don't get aggravated.

Speak to her consciously. Don't let your emotions get the best of you.

The door opened and she startled, her green eyes widening at the sight of me standing there all official-like in my uniform—apparently, officially mute.

I tried to pull words from my throat, but they wouldn't come.

I was too distracted.

Her pajama tank was nothing but a thin camisole, and the matching shorts left no more than two inches of her legs to my imagination. Her hair was down and wild, and her makeup-free face looked sleepy.

"Hey," I finally managed, forcing myself to man the fuck up. "Sorry to pop in on you without notice."

She waved it off with a little laugh. A *friendly* laugh I didn't think I'd ever heard from her before. "No problem. I was just napping."

Something was off. Something wasn't right. But my head felt so fucking fuzzy, and the thought of her in bed supported a physical reaction that took a whole lot of willpower to tamp down. It wouldn't have taken much to be noticeable in my uniform pants, and *for fuck's sake, Levi*, this was about more than that.

"Do you want to come in?" she offered. My heart abandoned my bid to calm down and sped up again as I nodded.

She swung a hand open in invitation, and I stepped inside.

The silence was deafening. We didn't speak, there was no TV on in the background, and for as audible as I felt like my heart should be, I couldn't hear it at all.

"Listen—" I started, ready to spill my fucking guts. The apology. The honesty. She deserved all of it.

But she spoke at the same time. And, as it turned out, it was a good thing that she did.

"Ivy will be home—"

Ivy. Ivy will be home.

Fucking *Ivy*.

Jesus Christ. This was *Camilla. Ivy's fucking twin whom you flirted with all day yesterday. No wonder she's smiling. No fucking wonder something feels off.*

I should've known the instant she'd opened the door. I should've seen it in the way her smile came too easy, the way her laugh was so damn friendly, and the way she didn't look at me like she was trying to figure out all of my fucking secrets.

And Jesus, what an even bigger asshole it made me that I'd forgotten all about Camilla.

"You go," she said with another, brighter smile.

Yeah, uh…no. I needed time to regroup. To figure out a new plan. To think of something innocuous and civil to say.

"No, no," I said faux-magnanimously, "You go ahead."

She giggled, and my chest tightened. Holy hell, I'd created quite the situation for myself.

"I was saying Ivy will be home soon. She ran over to the store to get some eggs." She shook her head ruefully. "The girl is crazy about her eggs in the morning, and I *might* have eaten the last of them while she was at work today."

My smile was brittle as I tried to be politely distant. "Gotcha."

Melancholy slid into my veins, and the idea of teleportation and time machines had never sounded so good.

If Ivy wasn't here, I had no reason for being here.

Camilla moved quickly to the couch, moving pillows and blankets and tossing them to the side. "Here, come sit down. You were obviously at work all day. You must be tired."

I shook my head, but she bustled on. "Come on, take a load off. I'll get you something to drink."

I moved to the couch with a nod, if for no other reason than to move on from the debate over whether I should sit down or not. And I couldn't deny I was hanging on the hope of her admission that Ivy would be home soon.

She laughed and shoved my shoulder playfully when I put my ass to the cushion, but she didn't take it any further. My back was straight, my arms tensely resting on my knees, and I'd have to scoot another foot and a half to come into contact with the backrest. "Relax, would you?"

I grabbed her wrist as she moved away, suddenly resolute to get this over with. I needed to tell her I wasn't interested. That yesterday had been way too complicated to explain, but that I hoped we could be friends. That I'd come here looking for Ivy.

"Actually…I kind of need to talk to you."

She nodded seriously, my tone undeniable, and then took a seat next to me. "What is it? What's up?"

"About yesterday," I started, and she smiled immediately. At the reminder of how much I'd fucked myself, I could barely feel my throat to swallow.

I tried to turn the corners of my lips up.

"I—"

She launched herself all at once, the signal she received from my message coming in completely fucking wrong.

Her lips were on mine before I knew what to do, her ass was in my lap, and her knees were in the couch on either side of my hips. She put her hands into my hair and all her passion into her mouth, and my surprised grunt of a gasp was the perfect opportunity to slide her tongue inside.

Well, fuck.

CHAPTER TWENTY-THREE

Ivy

ALONE, EERIE POLICE CAR SAT GLARINGLY IN THE DRIVE TO MY HOUSE when I pulled up from my short trip to the store.

I'd gone without thought, needing my stupid eggs so that I didn't break superstition. It was random, the idea that eating eggs every day first thing in the morning would somehow affect my performance, but I'd been doing it for years. Innocent in its beginnings, eating eggs was something I'd done out of convenience on the first major motion picture I'd ever been a part of. When it opened to a boom at the box office, I'd grabbed on to whatever I could as a part of the reason and ran with it.

The eggs had become a security blanket.

But now, forced to confront the scene of a police car outside and my sister home alone, I realized how stupid I'd been.

All for fucking *eggs*.

Camilla looked just like me. Sure, there were nuances that the trained eye would notice, but not someone looking to do me harm. Malicious intent was almost never that controlled.

I shoved open my door and left the eggs behind, running wildly toward the house while my heart tried to come right up my throat. Double the intensity of vomit, tears formed in my eyes as I forced it to stay put.

I steeled myself in the last running steps it took to clear the stairs and the front porch, and I turned the knob with violent anticipation.

I was scared to death of what I'd find on the other side of that shabby little cabin's door, but the thought of not knowing wasn't even a consideration.

Careening inside on a near slide and expecting the worst, I held on to the knob for support—physical help to stop my momentum and a crutch to hold me on my feet.

And there was carnage, all right.

Bloody and beaten, my heart finally made its exit and landed lifeless on the floor.

My sister. And Levi fucking Fox.

Intertwined and *kissing*. His back to the couch. Her hands in his hair. Their open mouths tangled and her eyes closed in pleasure. Her legs spread and open in invitation from a very opportune spot on top of his hips.

Oxygen evaporated. My breath was jagged as I fought to bring it back, and a rush of tears hit me harder than a tidal wave.

It was all so unavoidable now, the emotion. I'd ignored it for weeks, pushing it to the back of my mind and promising to confront it later. But it was here now. The hate and the lust and the *very real* affection I'd felt for Levi, all mutilated with a sharp allied sword.

He'd captured me. My spirit and my spine, both had been finely developed over the span of my life to ready me for him.

He was tortured, and I was the salve. I just had to dance to his lead until he could see the truth. I'd honestly believed that.

You're a fool, Ivy.

Levi noticed me out of the corner of his eye and shoved Camilla back a foot, but the damage was already *so* painfully done.

My feet treaded at the ground like water, moving my body back toward the open door in an effort to stay afloat. The room was cloudy now, my eyesight long compromised by my tears, and a steady whoosh had formed in my ears.

I had to get out of there.

Moving as quickly as I could, I swiveled so that I could run straight ahead and launched myself right out the door, over the stairs of the porch, and onto the gravel drive. My toe caught, and I went down on a knee.

Fuck!

Tiny pricks and raging fire burst free, and I used the pain to stanch the flow of my emotional wound and got to my feet.

"Ivy!" Levi yelled, the sound of his feet pounding on the wood of the front porch.

I turned back, fury burning the back of my throat, leaving it raw to the sting of all my salty, swallowed tears. At the sight of him, silent pain was no longer an option. He jumped down to the driveway and charged me.

"I fucking get it!" I screamed, holding up a vehement hand to stop his approach. "The arguments, the blatant statements, the games... I should have gotten it from the beginning. You want to be rid of me!"

I heaved a breath, and he filled the tiny, quiet moment with a whisper. "Ivy."

Camilla stood shaking and confused as she looked on from the top of the stairs, but I had absolutely nothing left in me to give her. The broken boards of our fence would have to wait to be mended, and her innocence would be recognized later.

Right now, I only had the energy for Levi.

"Well, congratulations. You got it!"

He closed his eyes, so I did the same, unwilling to torture myself with the sight of him any longer. The words would be all the visual either of us needed.

Words final and true, I bore the blow of each syllable as I spoke. After tonight, *Levi and Ivy* would never be a thing. And I'd have to find a way inside myself to get over what might have been.

"You're liberated of me," I whispered through a throat full of torturous gravel. "I..." I swallowed a thick ball of saliva and used it to wash away the grit, smoothing the edges of my message and outlining each declaration deliberately. I didn't want him to have any room for confusion and questions—I didn't plan to stick around to answer them.

"I'm *done* thinking of you when you're nearby and when you're not. I'm done tying myself in knots over your pain and your past. I'm done entertaining the idea that you're something other than you are, and I'm *done* with *this*." I jerked a wild finger back and forth between us. "This *twisted* thing between us—whatever it is—it's over."

CHAPTER TWENTY-FOUR

Levi

"**T**HIS *TWISTED* THING BETWEEN US—WHATEVER IT IS—IT'S OVER."

Ivy's words barreled out of her lips like a bullet from a rifle in the otherwise silent Montana air. They ricocheted, echoing and booming and filling the space around me so raucously the effect nearly brought me to my knees.

My heart clenched so hard inside my chest I thought it might migrate up my throat and choke me.

I wanted to go to her.

I wanted to wrap her up in my arms and kiss her pain away—kiss *our* pain away.

But we'd proven time and again that kisses couldn't heal real problems. In this instance, I was certain it would only worsen them.

She so obviously wanted distance from me. If she could have put a thousand miles between us with a snap of her fingers, she would have snapped twice to put two.

I rubbed roughly at my chest with one hand, trying to erase the phantom pain taking up residence beneath my ribs. It wasn't a turn in health, but an awakening of emotion that made me feel like I couldn't breathe.

stone

"Ivy," I called to her. I had no other words, no explanation, nothing of value that would ease her pain or fix what I'd just broken, but I had a million poor substitutions I was willing to try.

With a mane of red hair blowing in the brisk wind and green eyes harsh with accusations and something I feared was hate, Ivy stared at me from the yard of Grace's house.

Even tear-stained and raging, she was so beautiful it hurt. And now that I'd let the dam burst, the real, raw emotion I felt for her free to flow, I knew she held the power to destroy me.

God, how in the fuck had I gotten here? How had *we* gotten here?

Two good people battered and destroyed by a battle to survive one another.

Suddenly, I mourned for the mess I'd made of something I'd never really had.

Pain bit into my skin and forced my eyes closed.

I'd fucked up so bad. Not intentionally, but I'd played the starring role in this. I'd charmed her sister into thinking that kissing me was an option. And I'd spent so much energy trying *not* to feel something for Ivy, that it was too easy for her to believe I *didn't*.

Regret washed over me like long, slow waves on a shallow beach. Each wave was icy cold and sent shivers down my spine. I longed to go back and take a different path, but now that was impossible. The past was irrevocable. I knew that better than most.

I stared down at the ground and found myself envying the pebbles of the driveway, hard and lifeless and unable to feel torment. Unable to bleed and regret—unable to cry as they buried people they loved.

Ivy moved toward her car, but before she could swing open the door, I jumped into action. Hand hard and swift, I planted it into the glass of the driver's-side window and slammed it the few inches back to shut.

Her green eyes flashed to mine, agony and loathing mixing to make them muddy and toxic.

"Get out of the way, Levi," she spat.

I shook my head. "No. I can't let you leave like this."

"Get. The. Fuck. Out. Of. My. Way." Each word existed in a swirl of defiance behind gritted teeth, but I didn't falter.

I couldn't let her get behind the wheel when she was so obviously affected. It wasn't safe, and if something happened to her, I didn't know how I'd be able to live with myself.

I couldn't bear the thought of living in a world without her in it.

She'd become the fire in my veins. The instant she'd stepped her beautiful, stubborn, determined ass into Cold, Montana, she had turned my world upside down. She'd pushed my boundaries, and instead of fading into numbness and oblivion, I'd actually started to live.

I. Needed. Her.

I just wished I would've realized it sooner, before now—before I'd destroyed everything.

"Ivy, I can't let you drive right now," I said evenly, trying for once to be the calm one of the two of us. She flinched, the change in my demeanor unwelcome and ill-advised.

To Ivy, my late arrival to gentle consideration was an insult to all of the weeks she'd spent trying to evoke it.

"Fuck you, Levi!" she screamed, and without warning, she lifted her hand and slapped it hard across my face.

My skin stung from the assault, tingles and needles dotting the corner of my eye thanks to the new pressure in my cheek, but I didn't care. I deserved this. I deserved every bit of her anger. And her anger was better than nothing at all.

But my lack of response only urged more rage to boil inside of her.

It spilled over in the form of another slap to my face.

And another.

And another.

I lost count after five. And with each smack of her hand to my battered cheek, her tears turned to sobs.

Fuck. She was broken, and I was to blame.

Thick-throated and disappointed in myself, I gave in. The pull, the want, the need—it was real. I couldn't let it go on like this any longer. Wrapping my arms around her like a vise, I fought the pressure of her antagonistic body and pulled it to my chest.

For a brief moment, she allowed it, even burying her face and tears into my shirt.

"I'm so sorry," I whispered into her ear. "I'm so sorry, Ivy. What happened back there isn't what you think. It's the complete opposite, actually."

Instead of soothing the wound, my words served as a stabbing reminder of my indiscretions.

With a hard shove, she pushed me away, her eyes wet and pained and oh so fucking beautiful I felt it all the way to my bones.

"Your apology means shit," she said. "I don't want your fucking excuses or anything, for that matter! I'm. Fucking. Done. With. You!"

Done with me.

I wished I could go back in time, rectify my mistakes, take back all of the cruel and thoughtless things I'd ever done or said to her. But I couldn't.

Instead, I settled for giving her what I could then. Jaw hard and heart aching, I stepped away from the door of her car and offered it to her.

She stomped around me and swung it open violently, her movements swift and sure. She was pulling away from the pain and building a wall in its place, and I could see it so acutely I felt superhuman.

In reality, I just recognized the signs. I'd been doing it within the walls of myself for years.

Hand to the handle and the barrier of the door at her disposal, I thought that'd be the last word I got to speak. "Just explain one thing to me, Levi," she ordered, her voice steely as she paused in the space between who we were and who we would be. "Why do you hate me so much?"

My response was immediate. "I don't hate you, Ivy."

"Then why do you act like *I'm* the enemy, and *everyone else* gets a pass?"

Her question held so much truth that nausea clenched my gut, and without even thinking, the words spilled out of my mouth.

"Because I want to be numb…and with everyone else, I can. But not with you," I whispered. "You make me feel too much."

Green eyes searching blue, she looked at me for a long moment, and I silently hoped by some miracle she'd understand. But I knew it was a pipe dream. There was so much she didn't understand, but it was because she didn't know—because I hadn't told her.

A tiny prickle of hope touched the bottom of my spine and locked my body as she moved back out of the door of the car and slammed it shut.

"You need to leave," she demanded, squashing it with the heel of her boot.

I looked on in devastation as she moved back toward the house, a wide-eyed and confused Camilla still standing on the porch looking down at us.

"And don't worry, Levi," she tossed over her shoulder. The coldness in her voice made me cringe. "You won't have to *feel too much* anymore because of me. I'm done."

Done.

I didn't want to be done. Not with her, not with us. Not with any of it.

It was in that very moment that I made a promise to myself.

I would never be done with Ivy Stone.

Not today. Not next month.

Not ten years from now. Not *ever.*

I wasn't going to let her go.

Ivy walked up the steps of the porch and into the house, and with one confused glance in my direction, Camilla followed her sister inside, shutting the door behind her as she went.

I stood in the driveway, the direction of my gaze unchanged.

I didn't know where to go from here or what I could do that would right the wrongs I'd done to her.

I held on tightly to the fact that I'd be seeing her soon.

Tomorrow morning, in fact. Bright and early for another production day on *Cold*.

We were going to try this again. Only this time, I'd spend my time proving I *wasn't* an asshole.

This isn't the end; this is just the beginning.

Levi and Ivy's story will continue in *Cold*, Book two in the Stone Cold Fox Trilogy.

COLD

BOOK TWO IN THE STONE COLD FOX TRILOGY

Ivy Stone came to Cold, Montana, to film a movie about The Cold-Hearted Killer.

What she didn't expect was to come face-to-face with a real-life killer.

Or that the killer would have his sights set on her.

**Note: As this book is darker in nature, some sensitive scenes and/or subject matter may be present.

CH Warning: Levi and Ivy's story will continue in Book Three—*Fox*.

FOX

BOOK THREE IN THE STONE COLD FOX TRILOGY

The final installment in the Stone Cold Fox Trilogy.

Two murders, two funerals, and Cold, Montana, is back in the news.

Levi Fox and Ivy Stone need to find a way to move on.

But the universe has other plans.

Plans they don't see coming at all…

Stay up-to-date with our characters and our upcoming releases by signing up for our newsletter on our website: www.authormaxmonroe.com/newsletter!

You may live to regret much, but we promise it won't be this. If you're already signed up, consider sending us a message to tell us how much you love us. We really like that. ;)

Follow us online:

Facebook: www.facebook.com/authormaxmonroe

Reader Group: www.facebook.com/groups/1561640154166388

Twitter: www.twitter.com/authormaxmonroe

Instagram: www.instagram.com/authormaxmonroe

TikTok: vm.tiktok.com/ZMe1jv5kQ

Goodreads:goo.gl/8VUIz2

ACKNOWLEDGMENTS

First of all, THANK YOU for reading. That goes for anyone who's bought a copy, read an ARC, helped us beta, edited, formatted, or found time in their busy schedule to help us out in any way.

We love you guys. Every single one of you. Your love, your support, your enthusiasm for our words is *everything*.

This series is so unlike anything we've written, and honestly, it came in like Miley Cyrus on a wrecking ball. And once Ivy and Levi told us their story, we had to drop everything and just write all the words. They've ingrained themselves so deep in our hearts, and we can't wait for you to read the rest of their wild, twisty, angsty, passionate, and so unbelievably emotional ride.

So, THANK YOU.

Thank for you reading.

Thank you for supporting us.

Thank you. Thank you. Thank you.

THANK YOU.

Without every single one of you, none of this would be possible.

All our love,

Max & Monroe

Made in United States
North Haven, CT
29 January 2023